EDGAR ALLAN POE

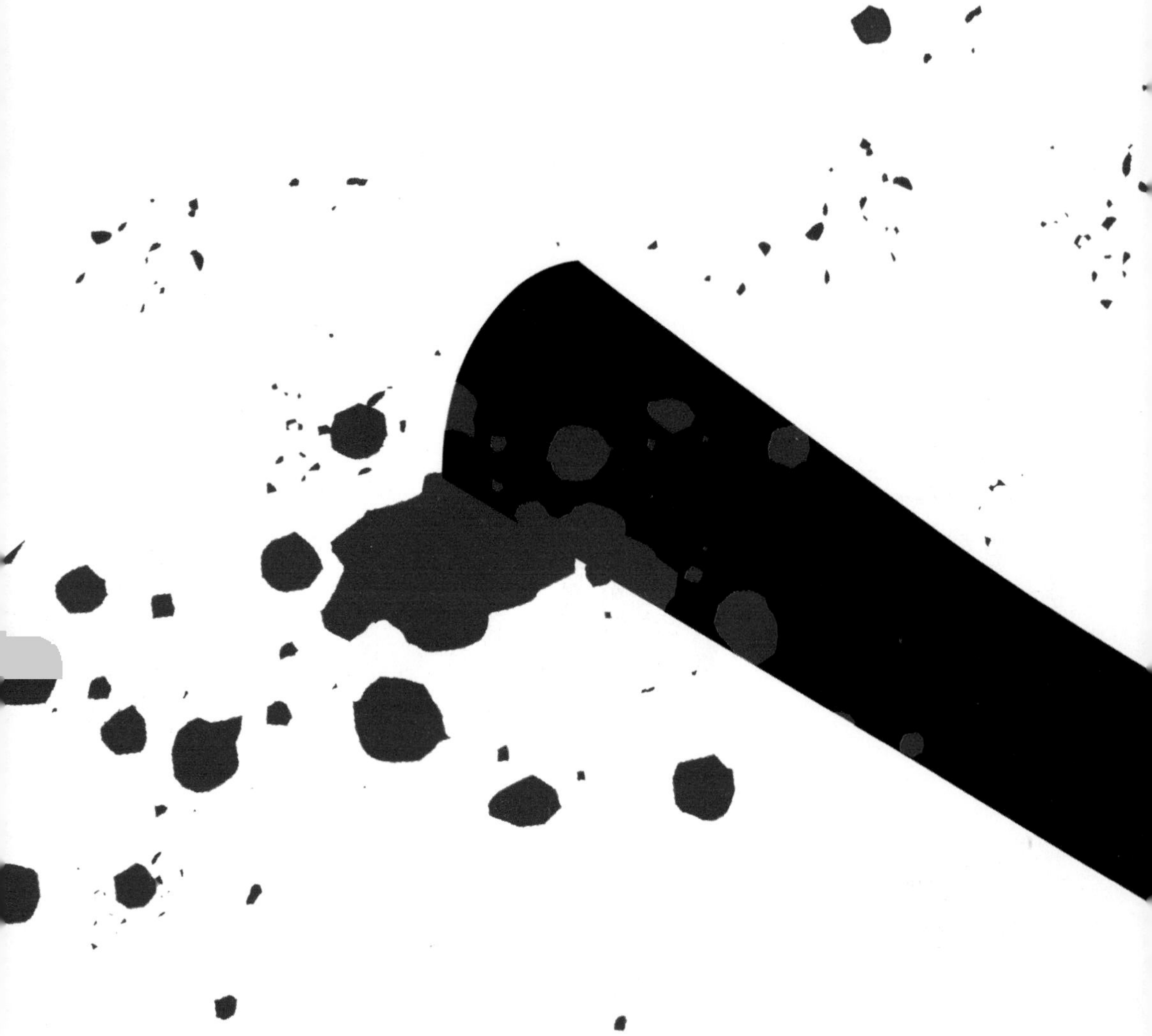

Edgar Allan Poe Graphic Novels
are published by Stone Arch Books,
A Capstone Imprint, 1710 Roe Crest Drive
North Mankato, MN 56003
www.capstonepub.com

Cataloging-in-Publication Data is available on the Library of Congress website.
ISBN: 978-1-4342-3033-1 (library binding)
ISBN: 978-1-4342-4259-4 (paperback)
ISBN: 978-1-4342-5966-0 (eBook)

Summary: There has been a murder. Two, in fact--and detective Auguste Dupin is on the case. With no leads, no suspects, and no clues, the case seems impossible to solve. However, Dupin is no ordinary detective. In fact, his explanation of the crime seems rather extraordinary. But it still happened, even it doesn't seem humanly possible...

Art Director: Bob Lentz
Graphic Designer: Hilary Wacholz
Edited by: Sean Tulien

Printed in the United States of America in North Mankato, Minnesota.
092012 006933CGS13

THE MURDERS IN THE RUE MORGUE

BY EDGAR ALLAN POE

RETOLD BY CARL BOWEN

ILLUSTRATED BY EMERSON DIMAYA

STONE ARCH BOOKS · CAPSTONE IMPRINT

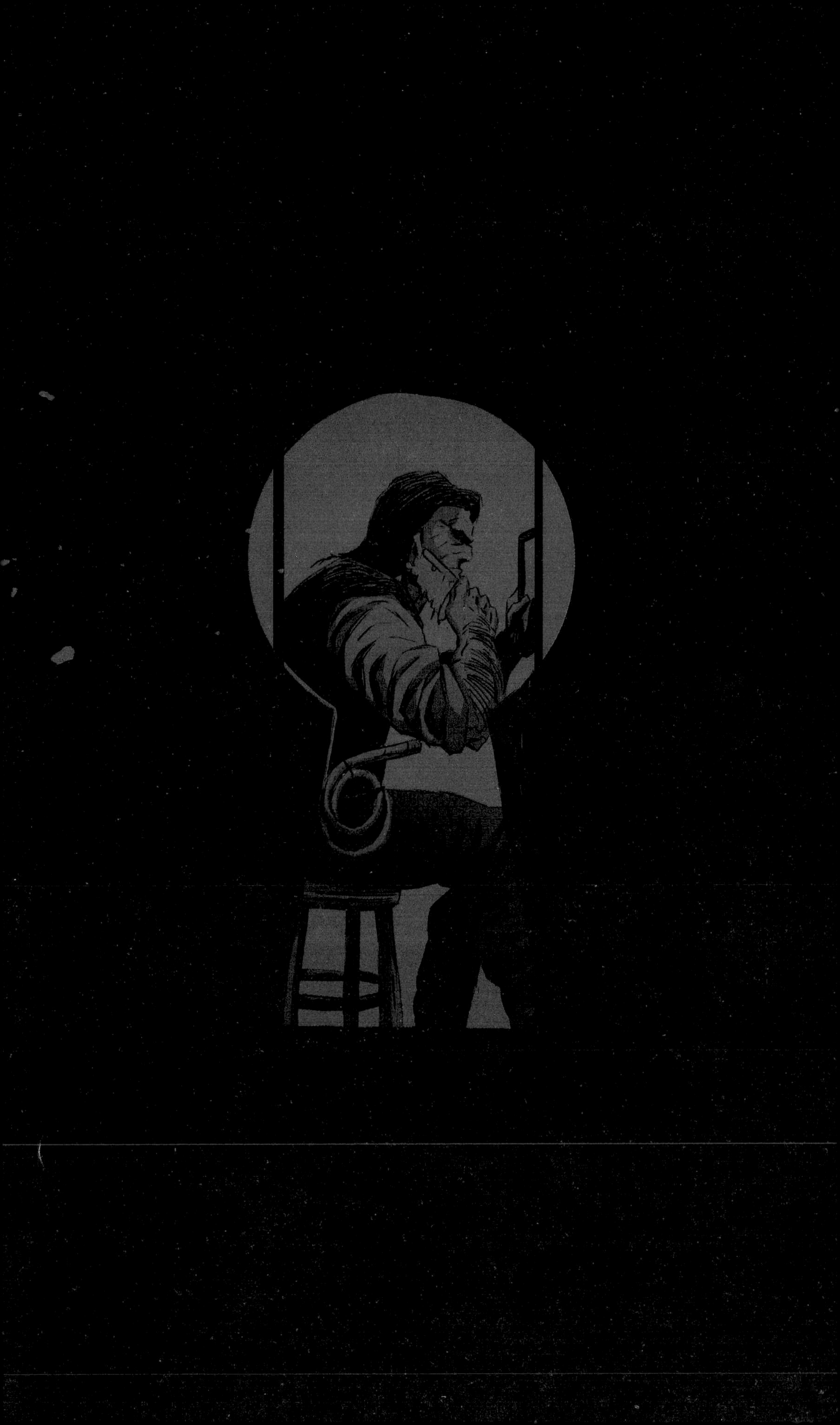

What songs the Syrens sang, or what
name Achilles assumed when he hid
himself among women, although puzzling
questions are not beyond all conjecture.

— Sir Thomas Browne, *Urn Burial*

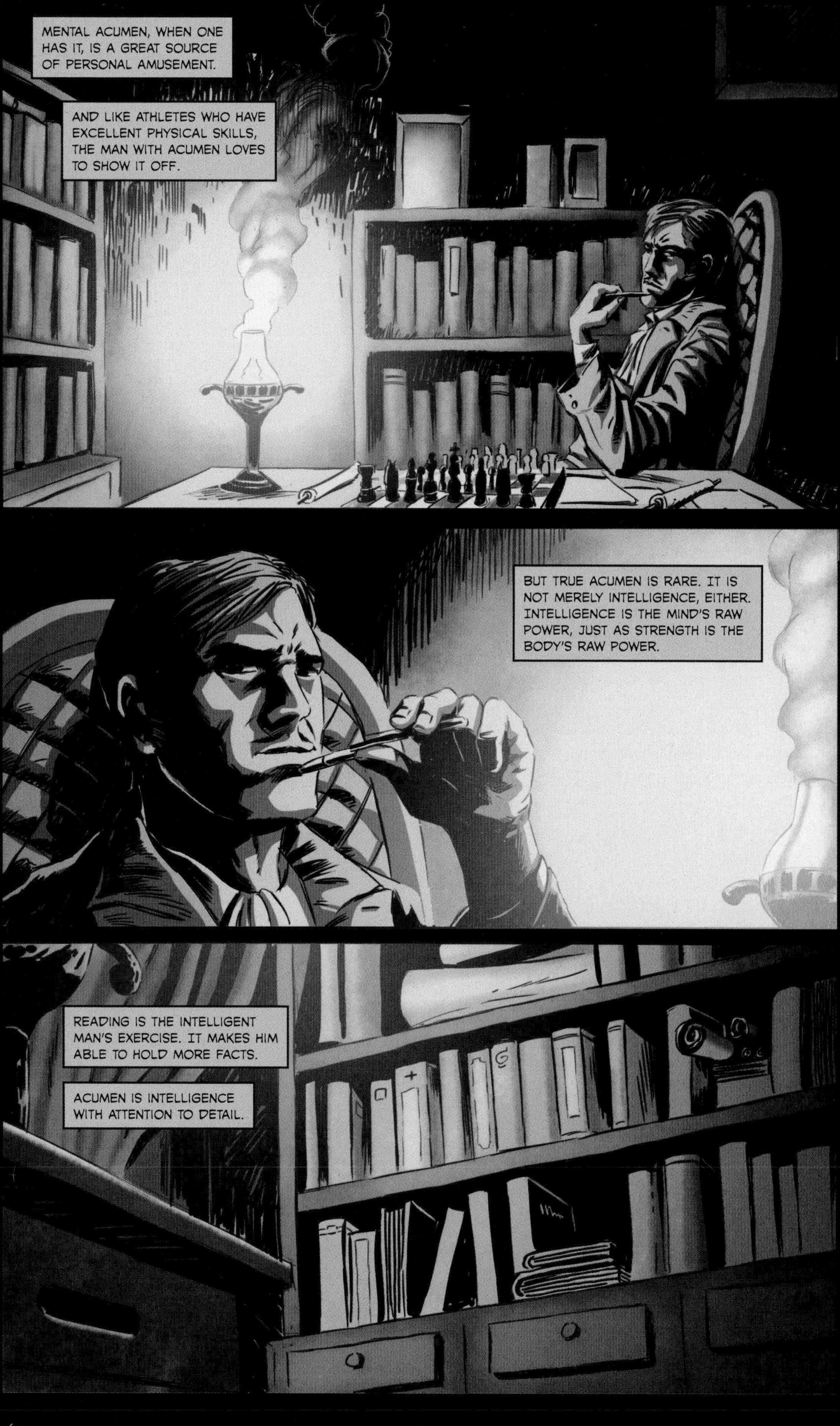
MENTAL ACUMEN, WHEN ONE HAS IT, IS A GREAT SOURCE OF PERSONAL AMUSEMENT.
AND LIKE ATHLETES WHO HAVE EXCELLENT PHYSICAL SKILLS, THE MAN WITH ACUMEN LOVES TO SHOW IT OFF.
BUT TRUE ACUMEN IS RARE. IT IS NOT MERELY INTELLIGENCE, EITHER. INTELLIGENCE IS THE MIND'S RAW POWER, JUST AS STRENGTH IS THE BODY'S RAW POWER.
READING IS THE INTELLIGENT MAN'S EXERCISE. IT MAKES HIM ABLE TO HOLD MORE FACTS.
ACUMEN IS INTELLIGENCE WITH ATTENTION TO DETAIL.

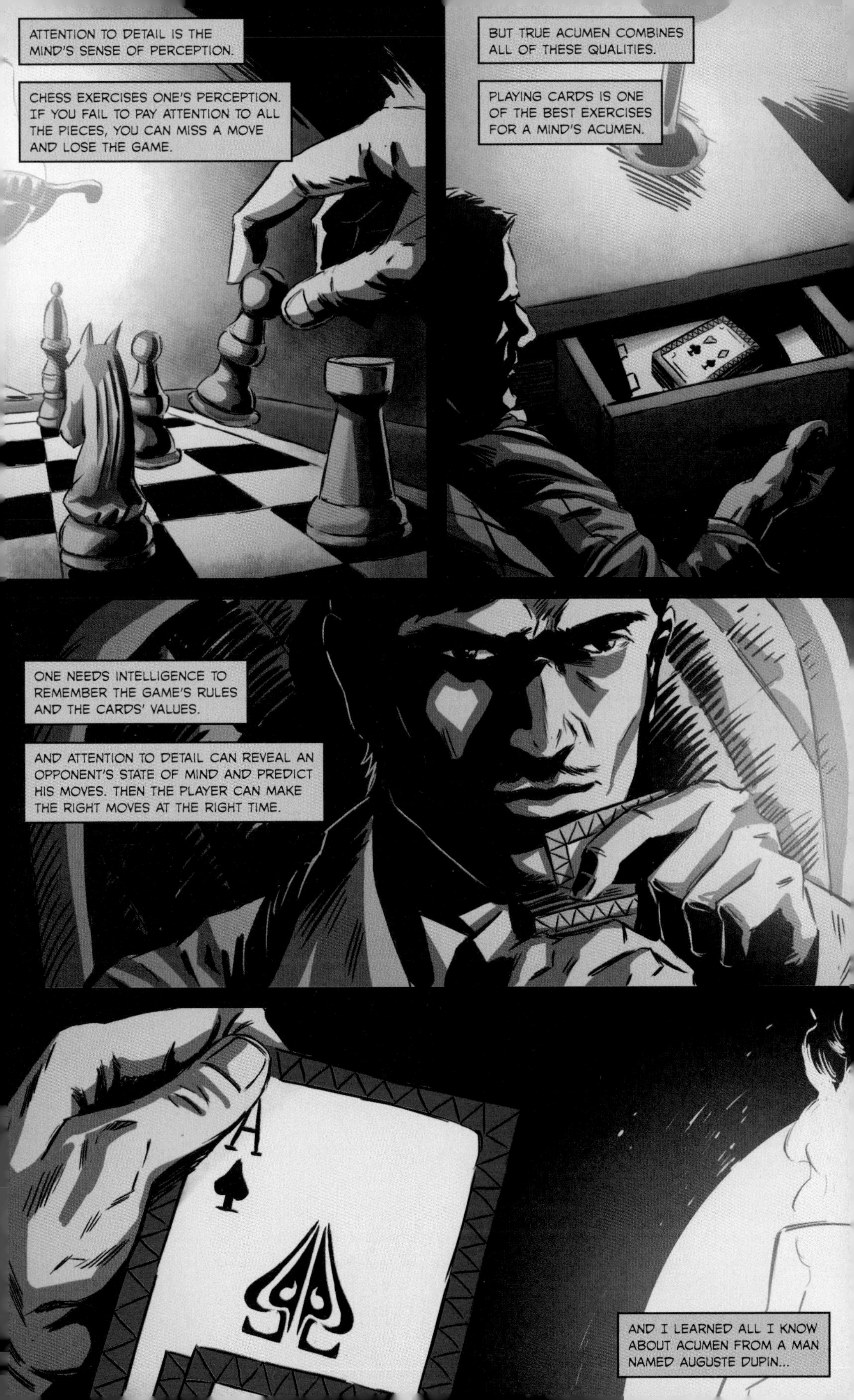
ATTENTION TO DETAIL IS THE MIND'S SENSE OF PERCEPTION.
CHESS EXERCISES ONE'S PERCEPTION. IF YOU FAIL TO PAY ATTENTION TO ALL THE PIECES, YOU CAN MISS A MOVE AND LOSE THE GAME.
BUT TRUE ACUMEN COMBINES ALL OF THESE QUALITIES.
PLAYING CARDS IS ONE OF THE BEST EXERCISES FOR A MIND'S ACUMEN.
ONE NEEDS INTELLIGENCE TO REMEMBER THE GAME'S RULES AND THE CARDS' VALUES.
AND ATTENTION TO DETAIL CAN REVEAL AN OPPONENT'S STATE OF MIND AND PREDICT HIS MOVES. THEN THE PLAYER CAN MAKE THE RIGHT MOVES AT THE RIGHT TIME.
AND I LEARNED ALL I KNOW ABOUT ACUMEN FROM A MAN NAMED AUGUSTE DUPIN...

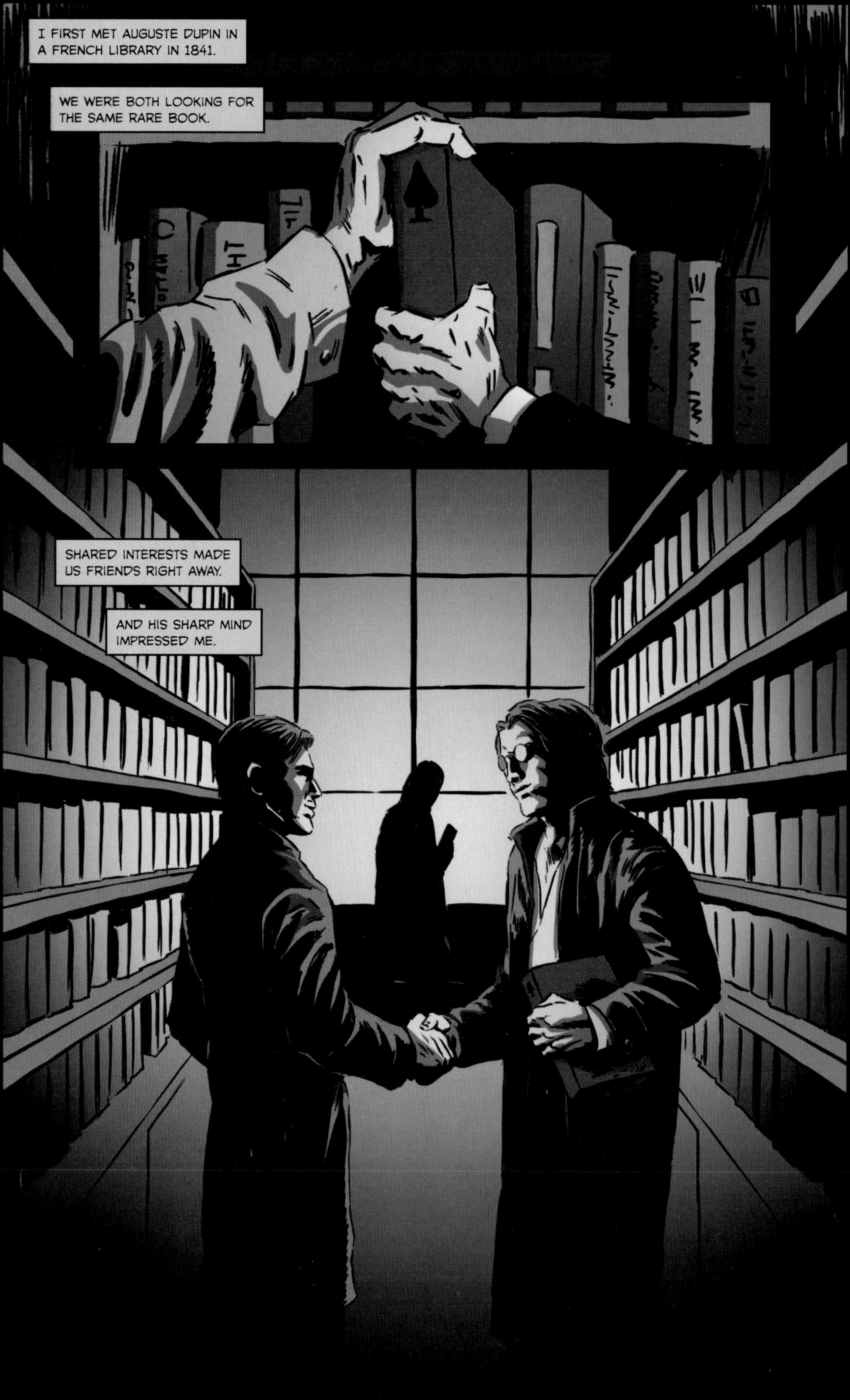
I FIRST MET AUGUSTE DUPIN IN A FRENCH LIBRARY IN 1841.
WE WERE BOTH LOOKING FOR THE SAME RARE BOOK.
SHARED INTERESTS MADE US FRIENDS RIGHT AWAY.
AND HIS SHARP MIND IMPRESSED ME.

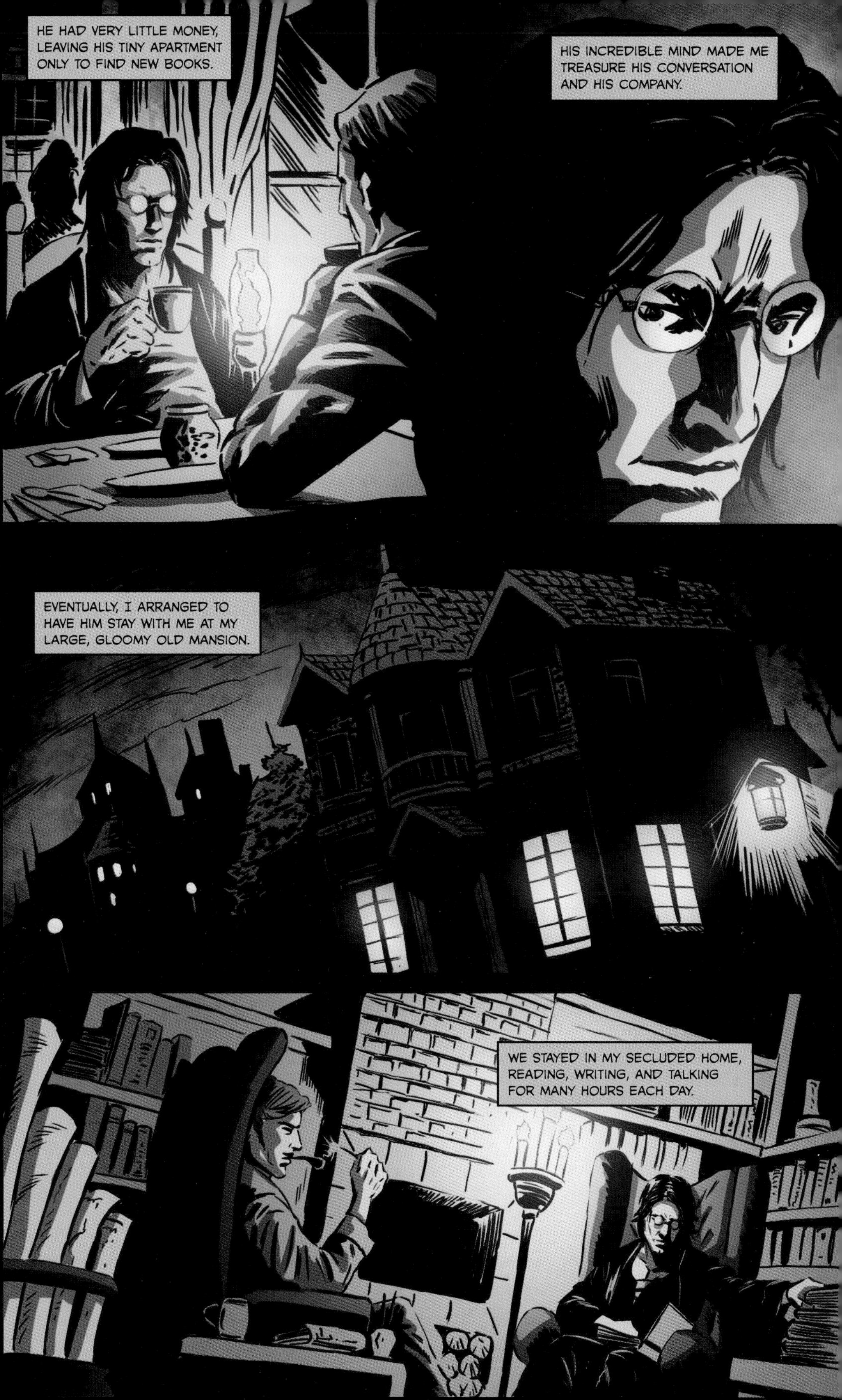
HE HAD VERY LITTLE MONEY, LEAVING HIS TINY APARTMENT ONLY TO FIND NEW BOOKS.
HIS INCREDIBLE MIND MADE ME TREASURE HIS CONVERSATION AND HIS COMPANY.
EVENTUALLY, I ARRANGED TO HAVE HIM STAY WITH ME AT MY LARGE, GLOOMY OLD MANSION.
WE STAYED IN MY SECLUDED HOME, READING, WRITING, AND TALKING FOR MANY HOURS EACH DAY.

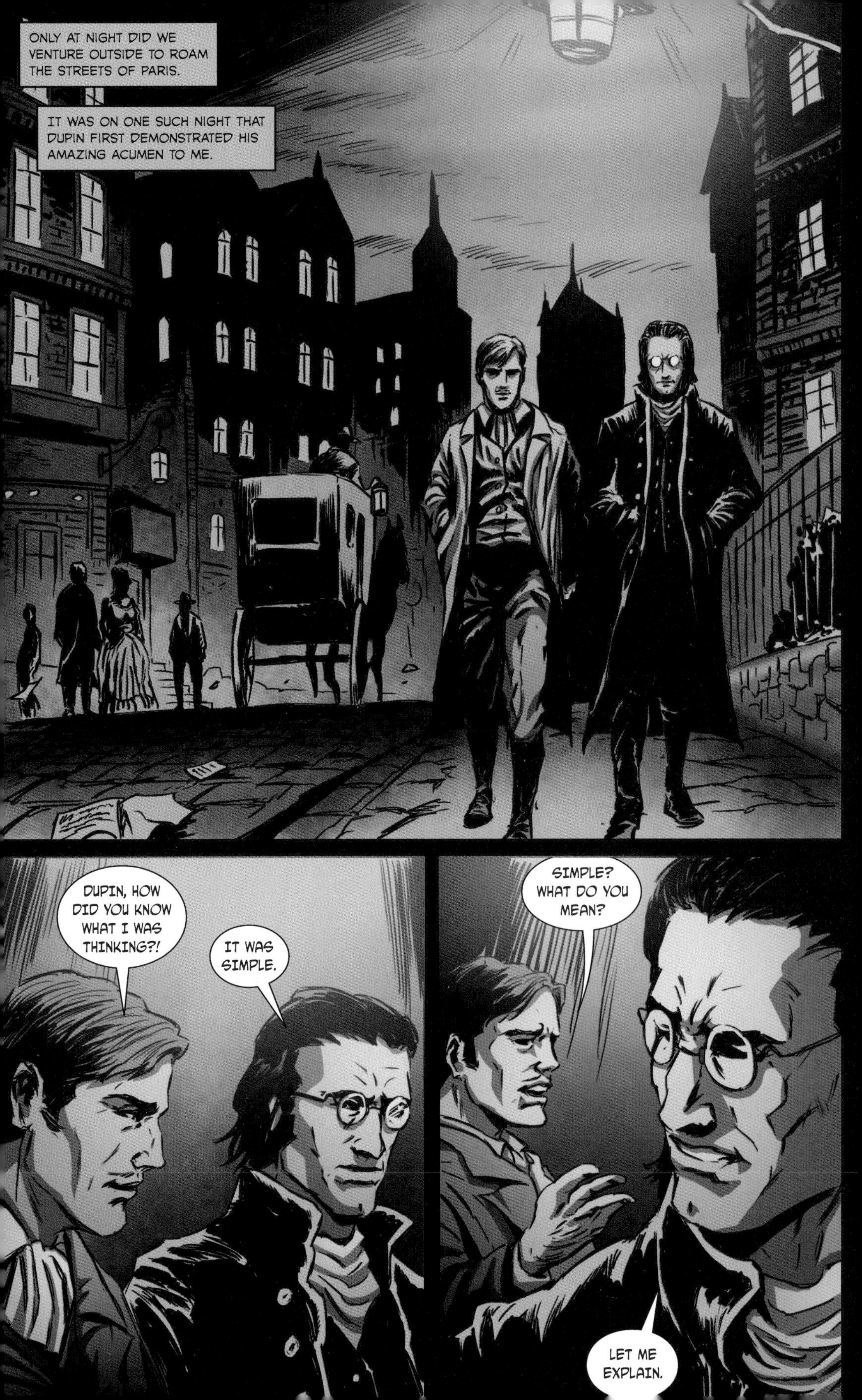
ONLY AT NIGHT DID WE VENTURE OUTSIDE TO ROAM THE STREETS OF PARIS.
IT WAS ON ONE SUCH NIGHT THAT DUPIN FIRST DEMONSTRATED HIS AMAZING ACUMEN TO ME.
DUPIN, HOW DID YOU KNOW WHAT I WAS THINKING?!
IT WAS SIMPLE.
SIMPLE? WHAT DO YOU MEAN?
LET ME EXPLAIN.

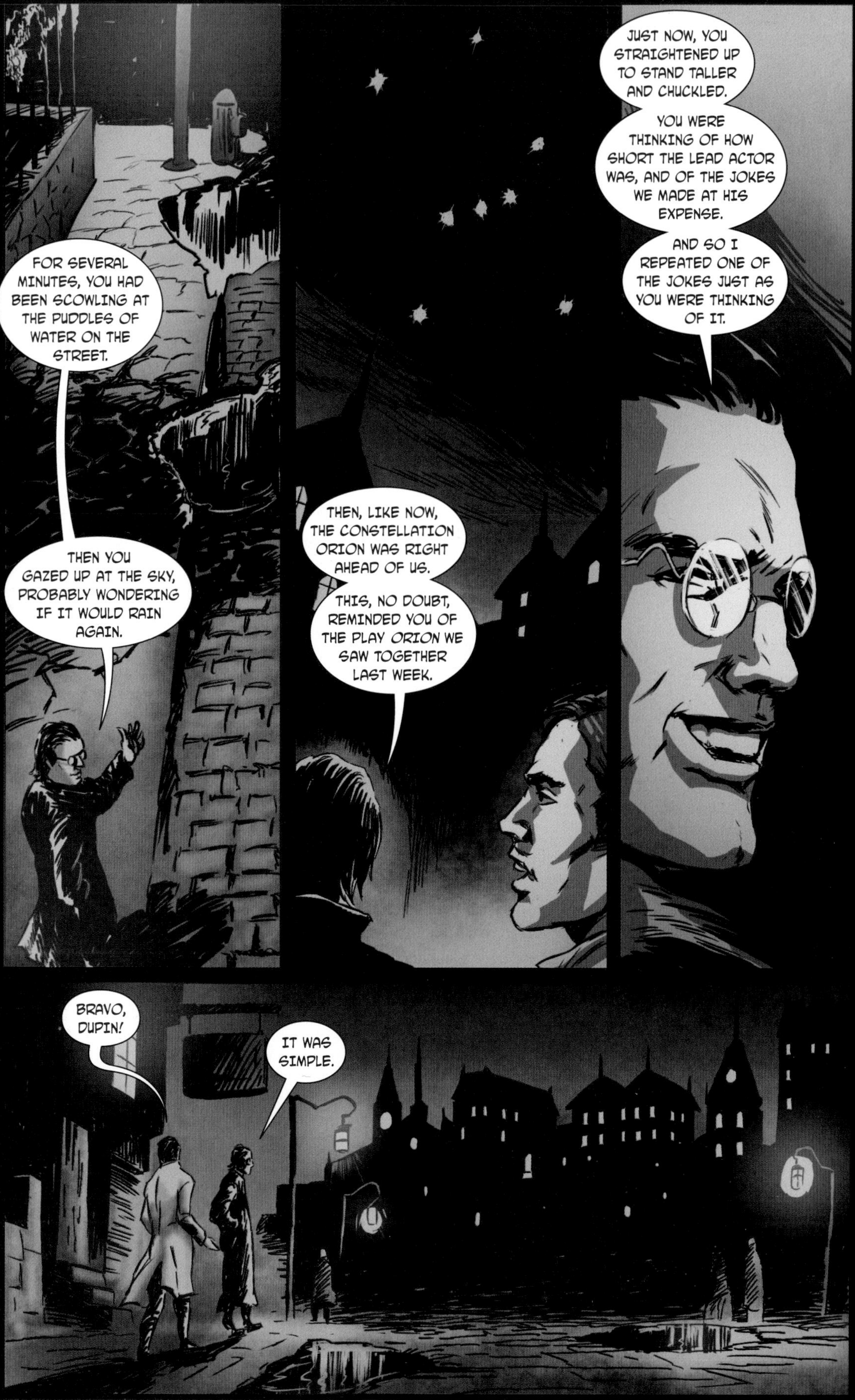
FOR SEVERAL MINUTES, YOU HAD BEEN SCOWLING AT THE PUDDLES OF WATER ON THE STREET.
THEN YOU GAZED UP AT THE SKY, PROBABLY WONDERING IF IT WOULD RAIN AGAIN.
THEN, LIKE NOW, THE CONSTELLATION ORION WAS RIGHT AHEAD OF US.
THIS, NO DOUBT, REMINDED YOU OF THE PLAY *ORION* WE SAW TOGETHER LAST WEEK.
JUST NOW, YOU STRAIGHTENED UP TO STAND TALLER AND CHUCKLED.
YOU WERE THINKING OF HOW SHORT THE LEAD ACTOR WAS, AND OF THE JOKES WE MADE AT HIS EXPENSE.
AND SO I REPEATED ONE OF THE JOKES JUST AS YOU WERE THINKING OF IT.
BRAVO, DUPIN!
IT WAS SIMPLE.

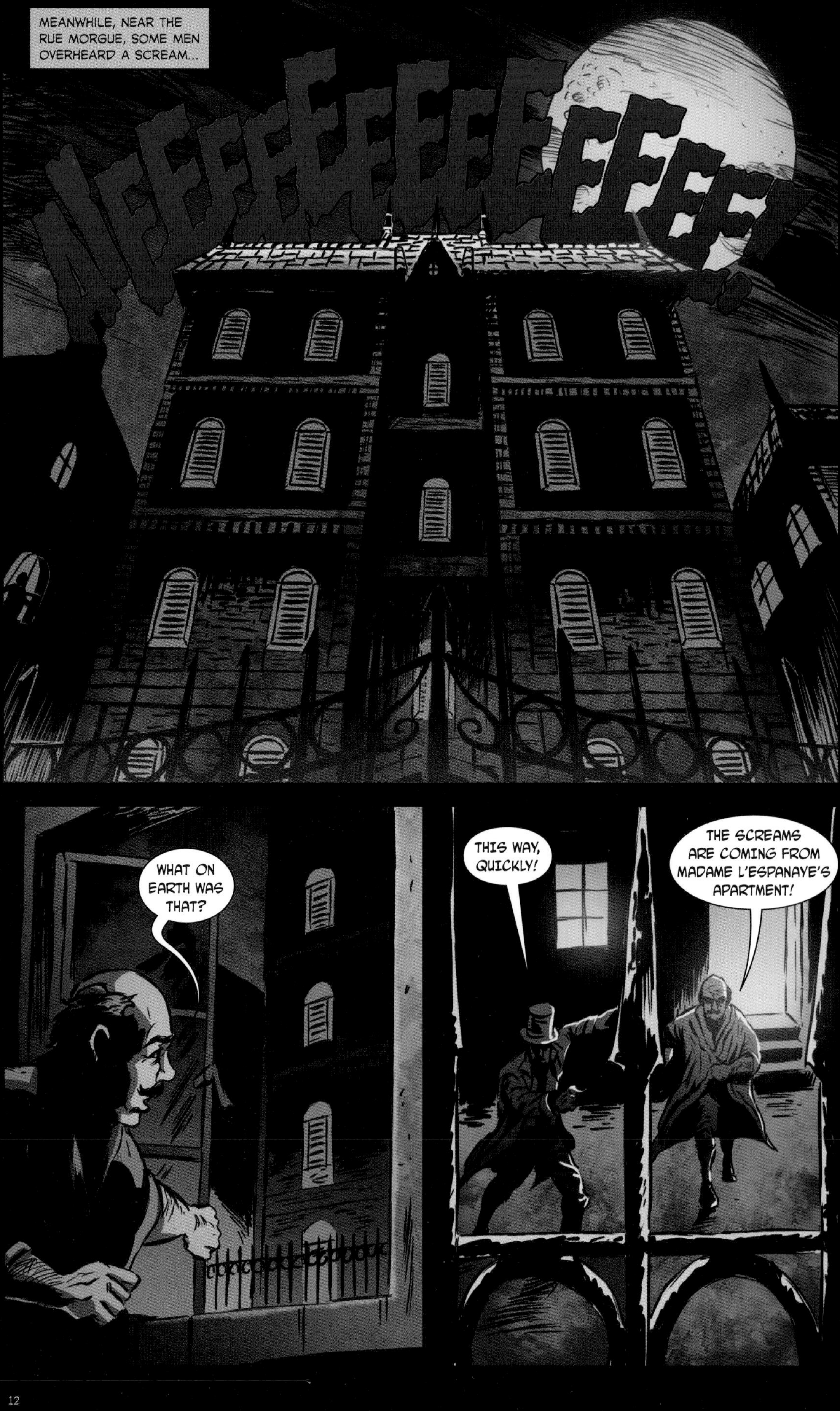
MEANWHILE, NEAR THE RUE MORGUE, SOME MEN OVERHEARD A SCREAM...
WEEEEEEEEEEEEEEE!
WHAT ON EARTH WAS THAT?
THIS WAY, QUICKLY!
THE SCREAMS ARE COMING FROM MADAME L'ESPANAYE'S APARTMENT!

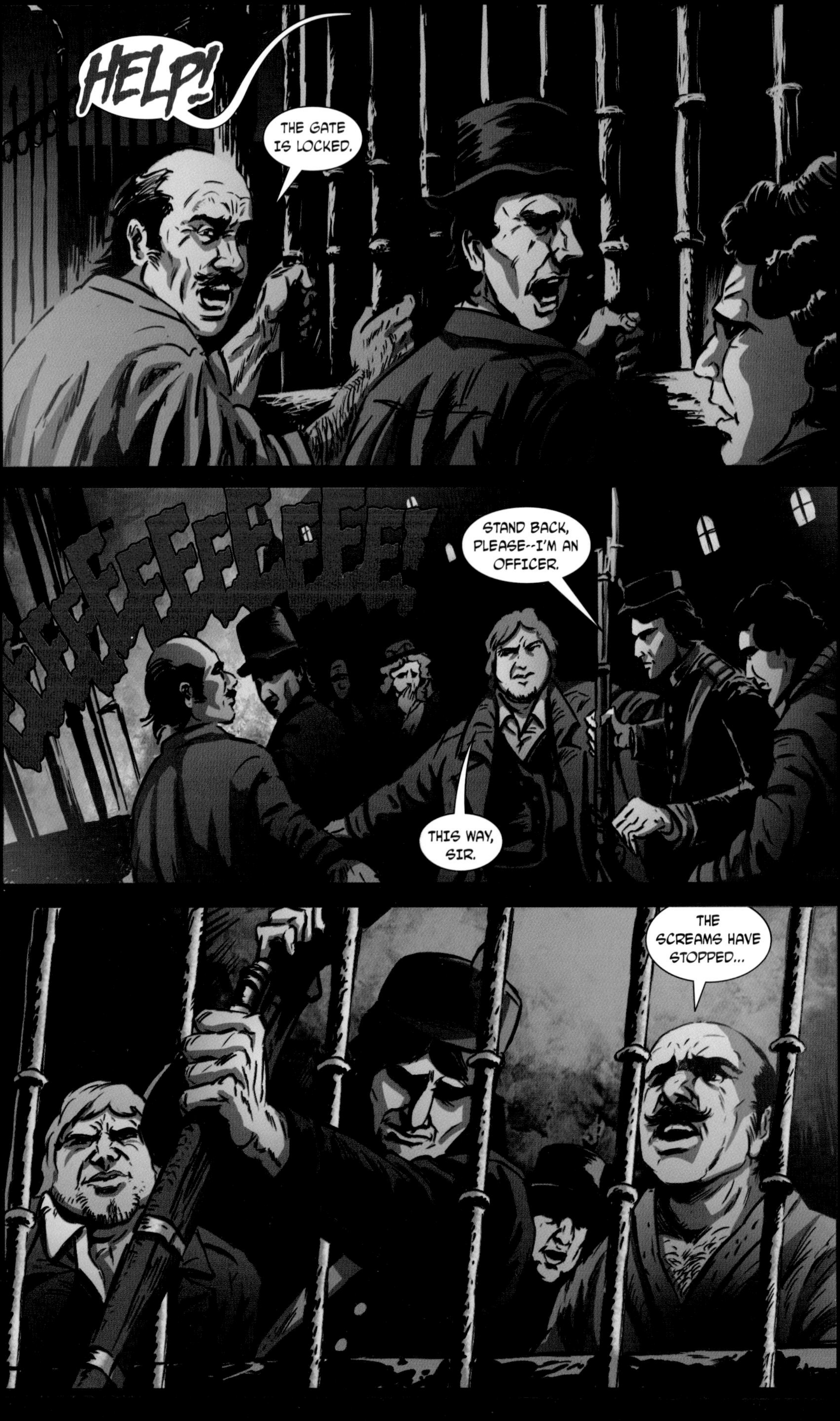
HELP!
THE GATE IS LOCKED.
STAND BACK, PLEASE--I'M AN OFFICER.
THIS WAY, SIR.
THE SCREAMS HAVE STOPPED...

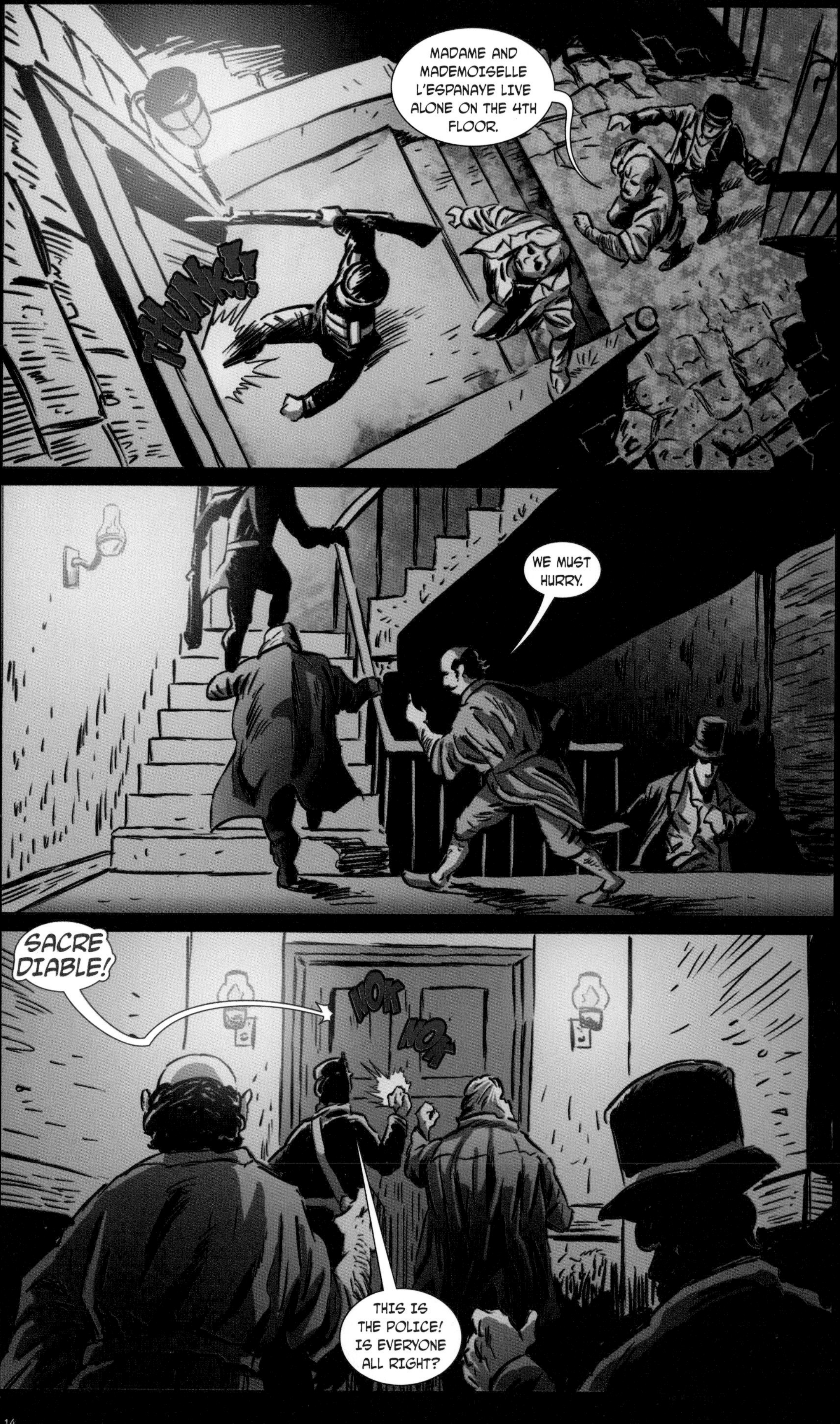
MADAME AND MADEMOISELLE L'ESPANAYE LIVE ALONE ON THE 4TH FLOOR.
THUNK!!
WE MUST HURRY.
SACRE DIABLE!
NOK
NOK
THIS IS THE POLICE! IS EVERYONE ALL RIGHT?

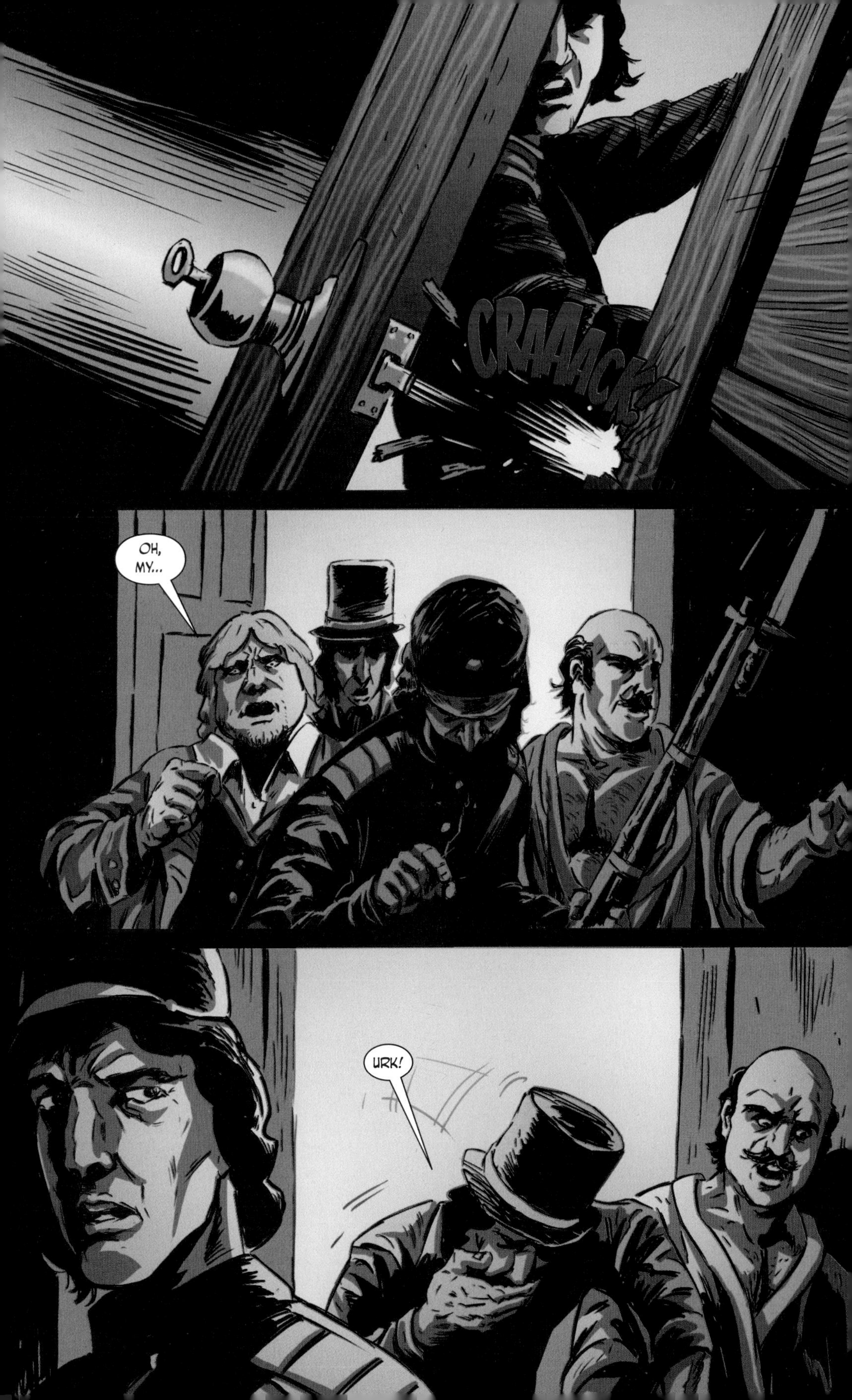
CRAAACK!
OH, MY...
URK!

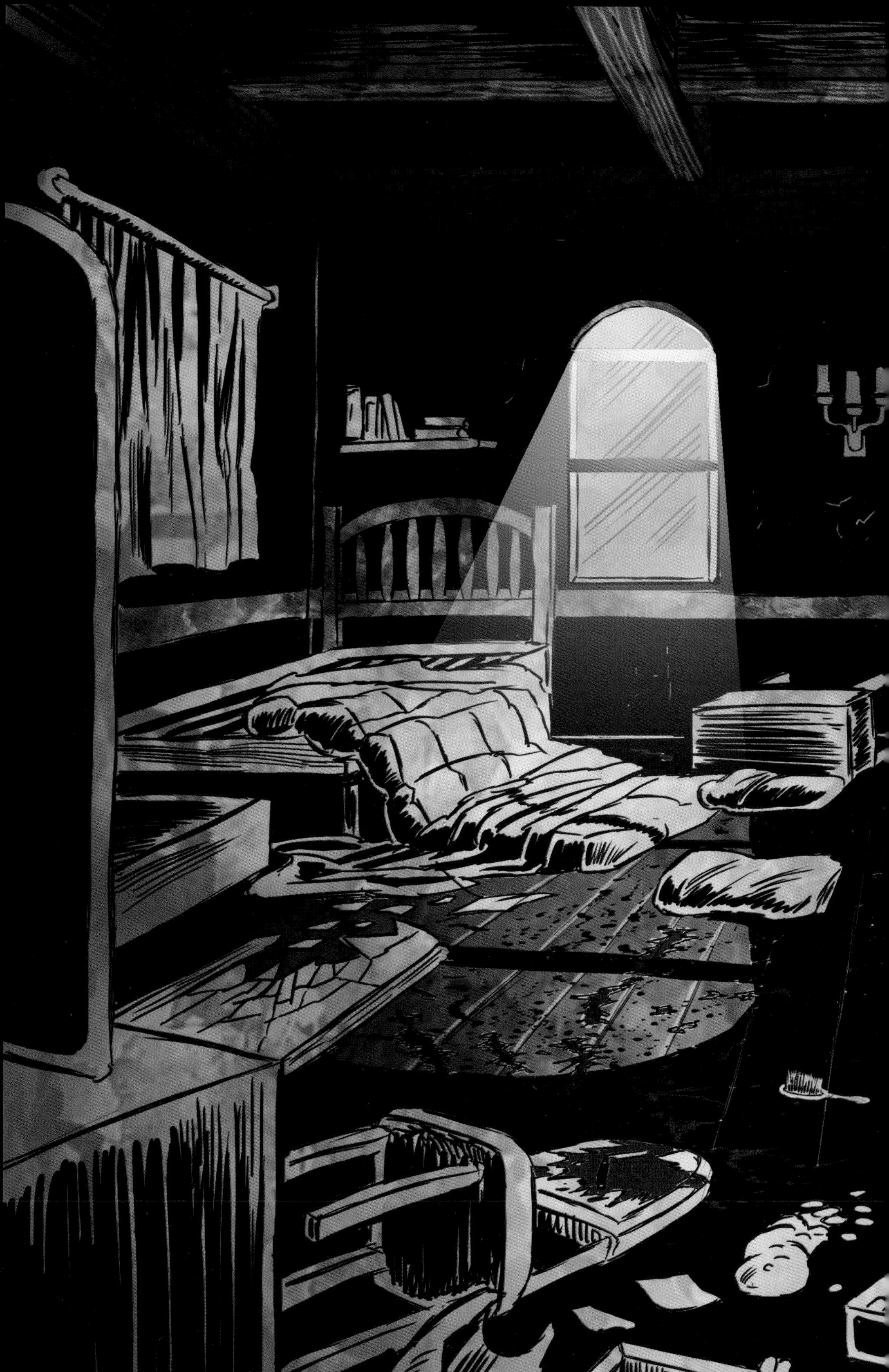

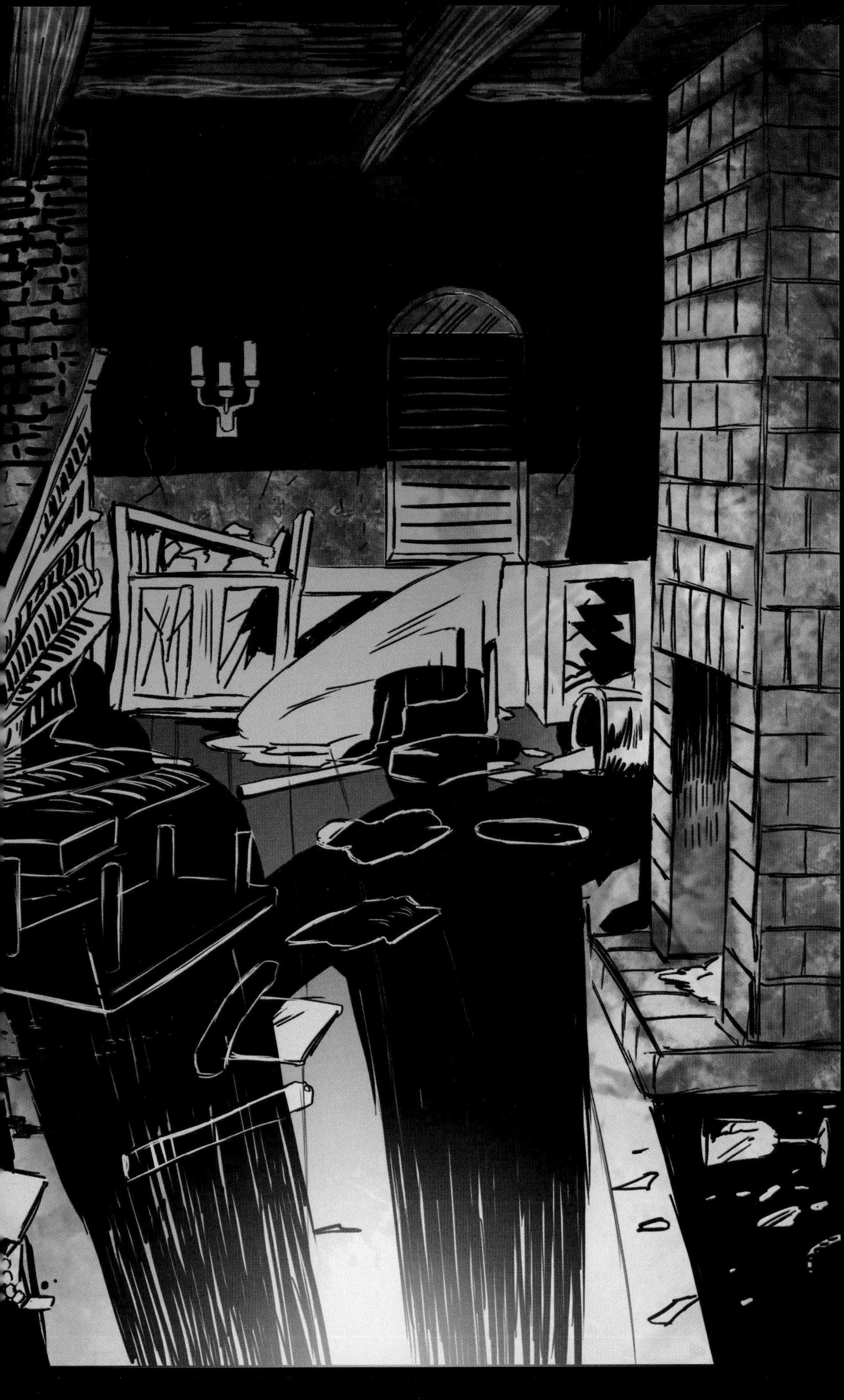

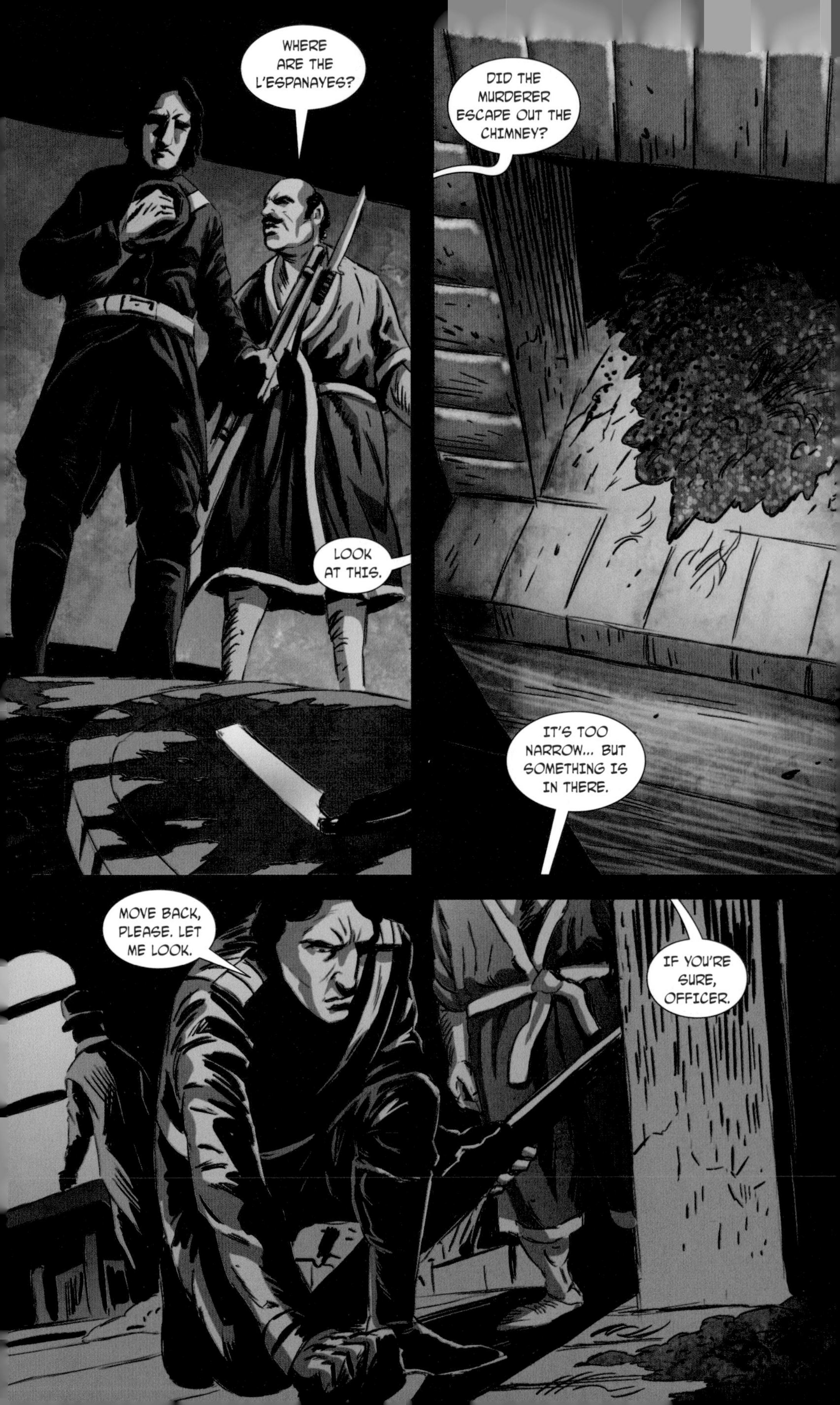
WHERE ARE THE L'ESPANAYES?
LOOK AT THIS.
DID THE MURDERER ESCAPE OUT THE CHIMNEY?
IT'S TOO NARROW... BUT SOMETHING IS IN THERE.
MOVE BACK, PLEASE. LET ME LOOK.
IF YOU'RE SURE, OFFICER.

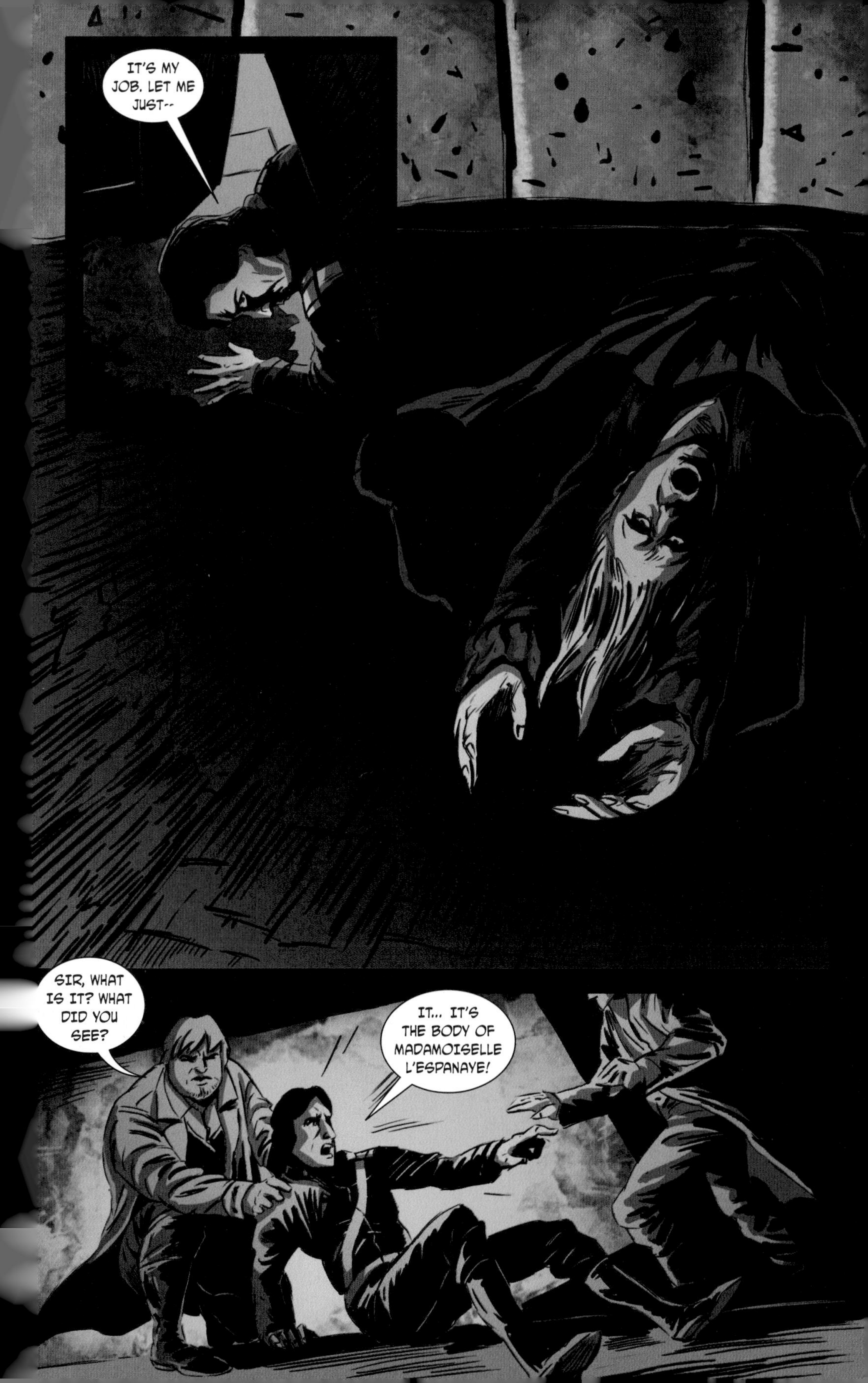
IT'S MY JOB. LET ME JUST--
SIR, WHAT IS IT? WHAT DID YOU SEE?
IT... IT'S THE BODY OF MADAMOISELLE L'ESPANAYE!

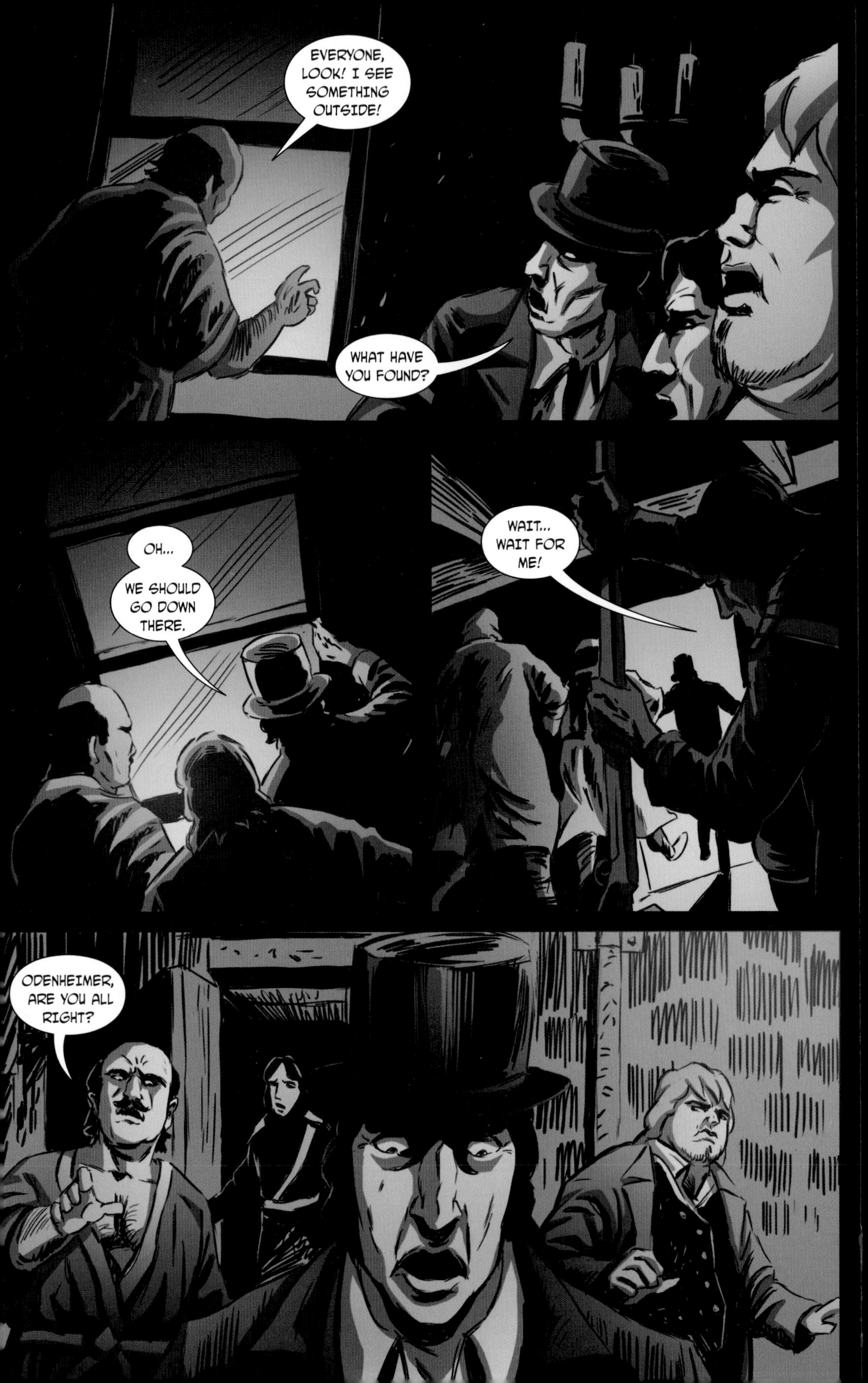
EVERYONE, LOOK! I SEE SOMETHING OUTSIDE!
WHAT HAVE YOU FOUND?
OH...
WE SHOULD GO DOWN THERE.
WAIT... WAIT FOR ME!
ODENHEIMER, ARE YOU ALL RIGHT?

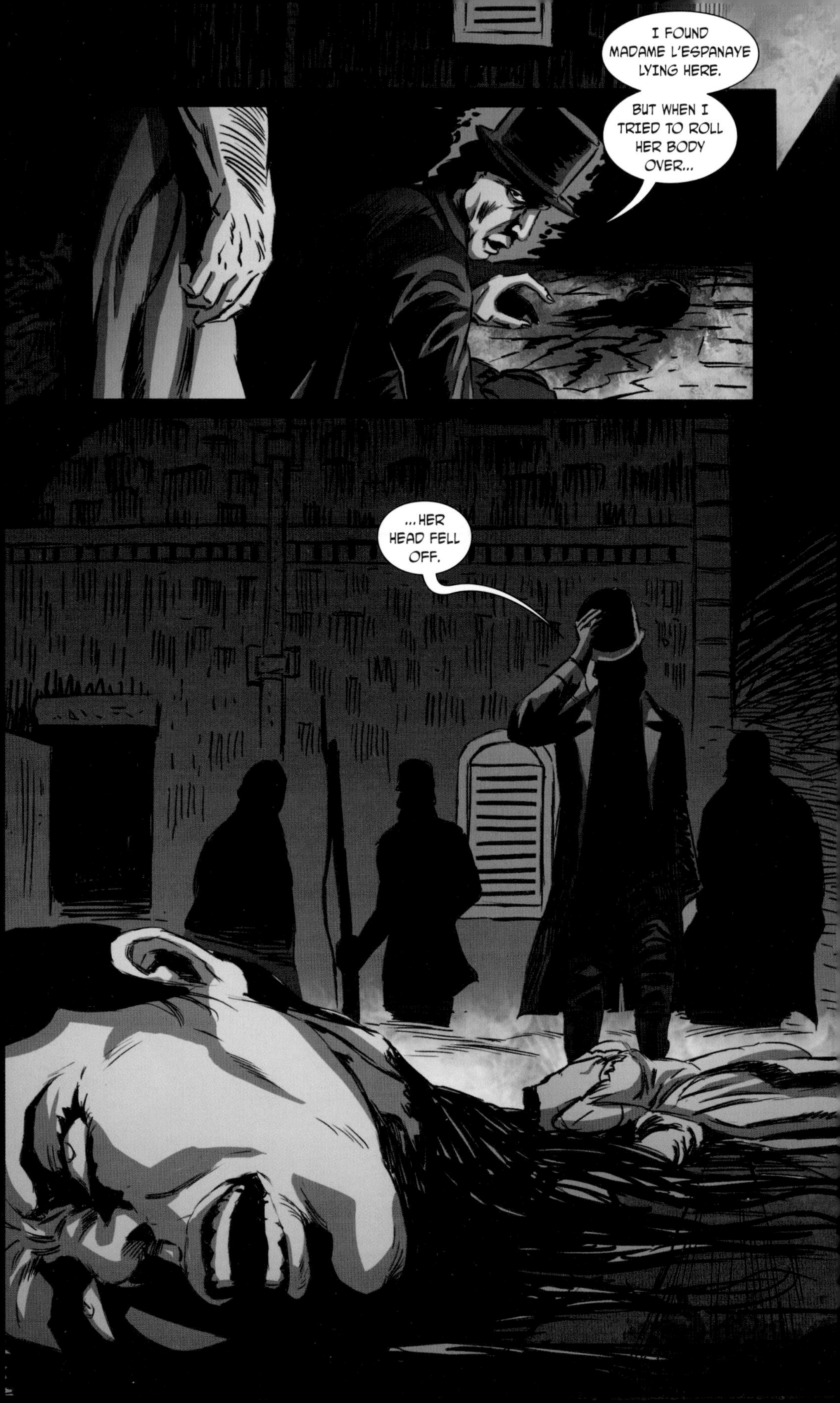
I FOUND MADAME L'ESPANAYE LYING HERE.
BUT WHEN I TRIED TO ROLL HER BODY OVER...
...HER HEAD FELL OFF.

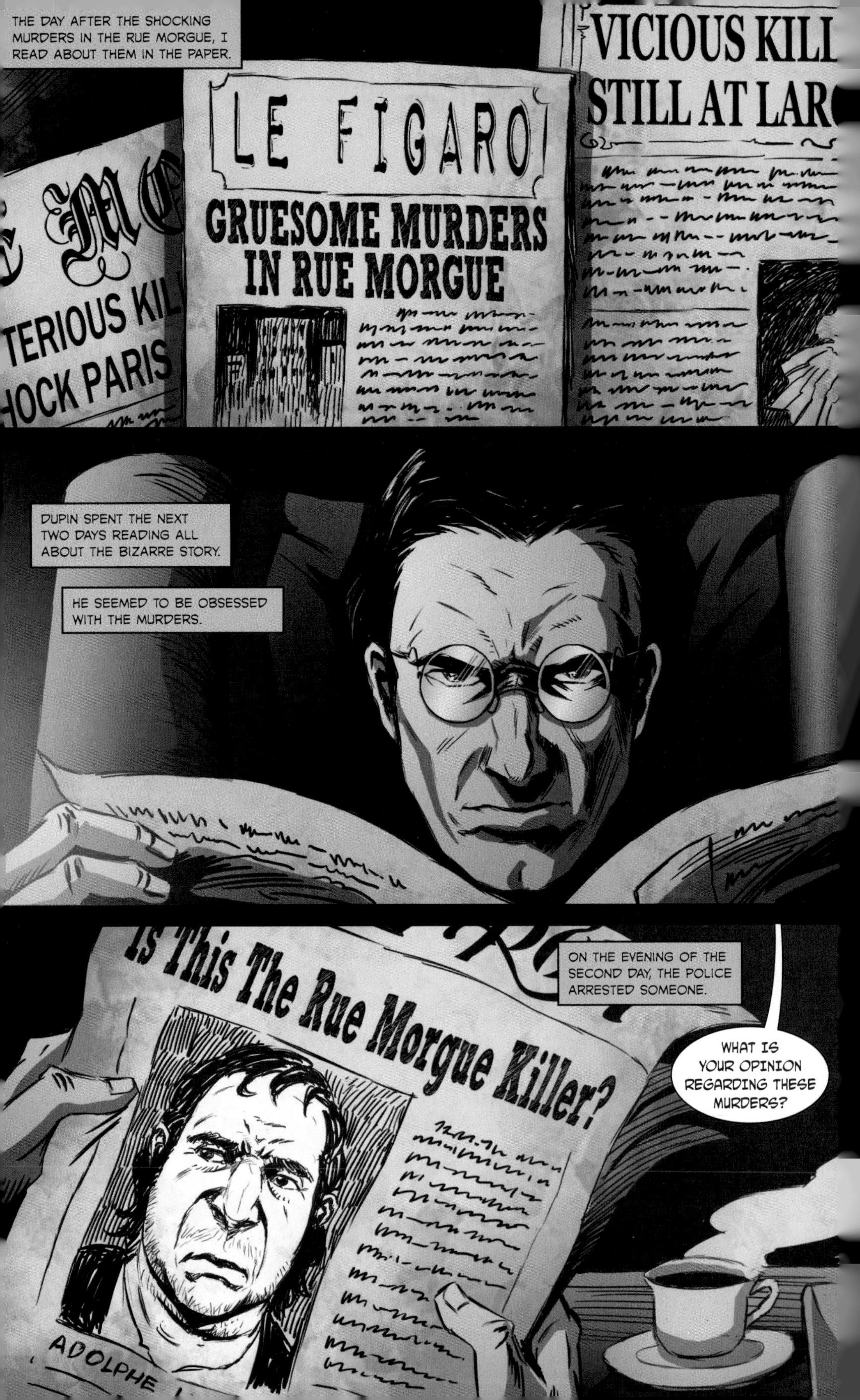
THE DAY AFTER THE SHOCKING MURDERS IN THE RUE MORGUE, I READ ABOUT THEM IN THE PAPER.
VICIOUS KILL
STILL AT LAR
LE FIGARO
GRUESOME MURDERS IN RUE MORGUE
TERIOUS KIL
HOCK PARIS
DUPIN SPENT THE NEXT TWO DAYS READING ALL ABOUT THE BIZARRE STORY.
HE SEEMED TO BE OBSESSED WITH THE MURDERS.
Is This The Rue Morgue Killer?
ON THE EVENING OF THE SECOND DAY, THE POLICE ARRESTED SOMEONE.
WHAT IS YOUR OPINION REGARDING THESE MURDERS?
ADOLPHE

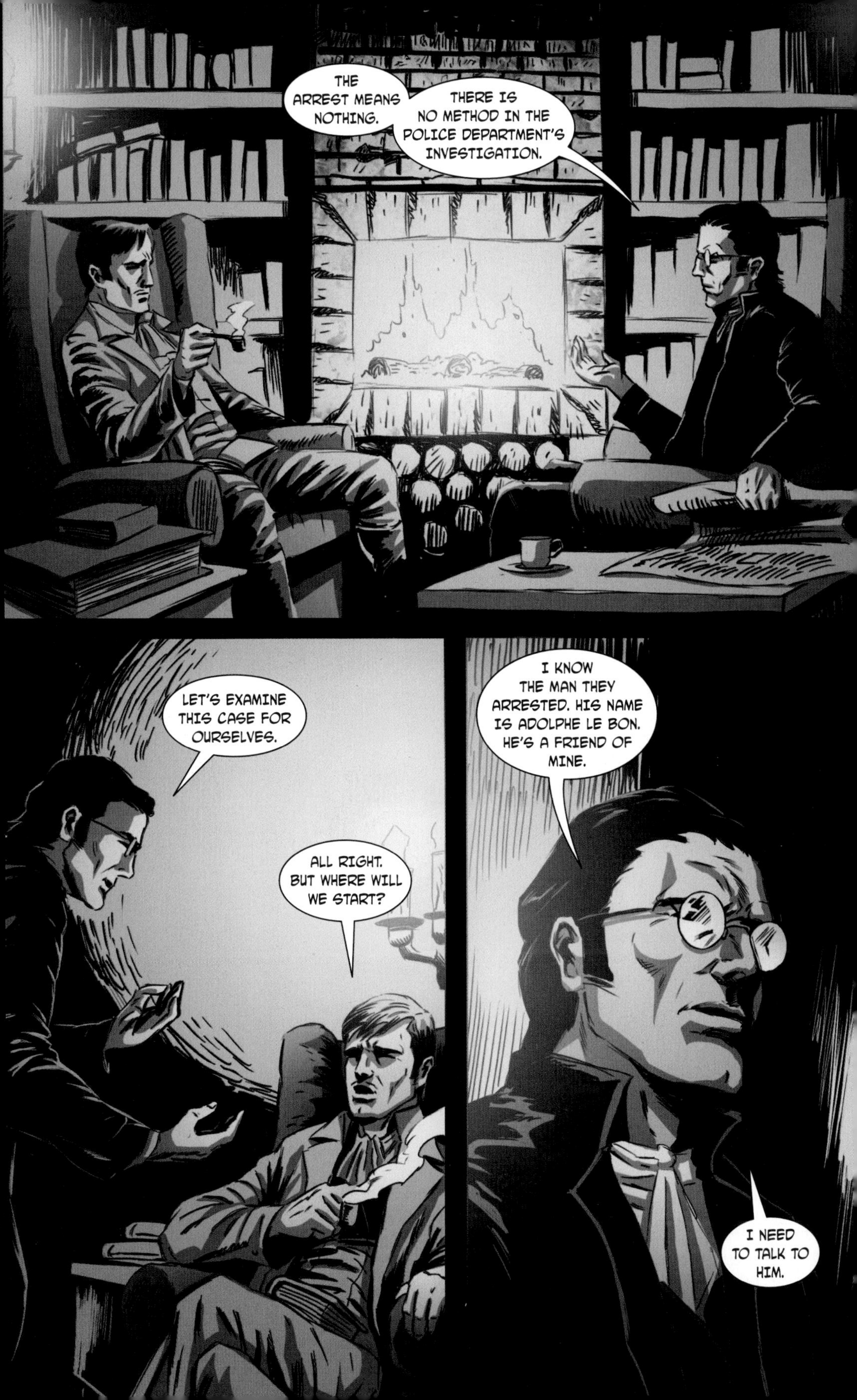
THE ARREST MEANS NOTHING.
THERE IS NO METHOD IN THE POLICE DEPARTMENT'S INVESTIGATION.
LET'S EXAMINE THIS CASE FOR OURSELVES.
ALL RIGHT. BUT WHERE WILL WE START?
I KNOW THE MAN THEY ARRESTED. HIS NAME IS ADOLPHE LE BON. HE'S A FRIEND OF MINE.
I NEED TO TALK TO HIM.

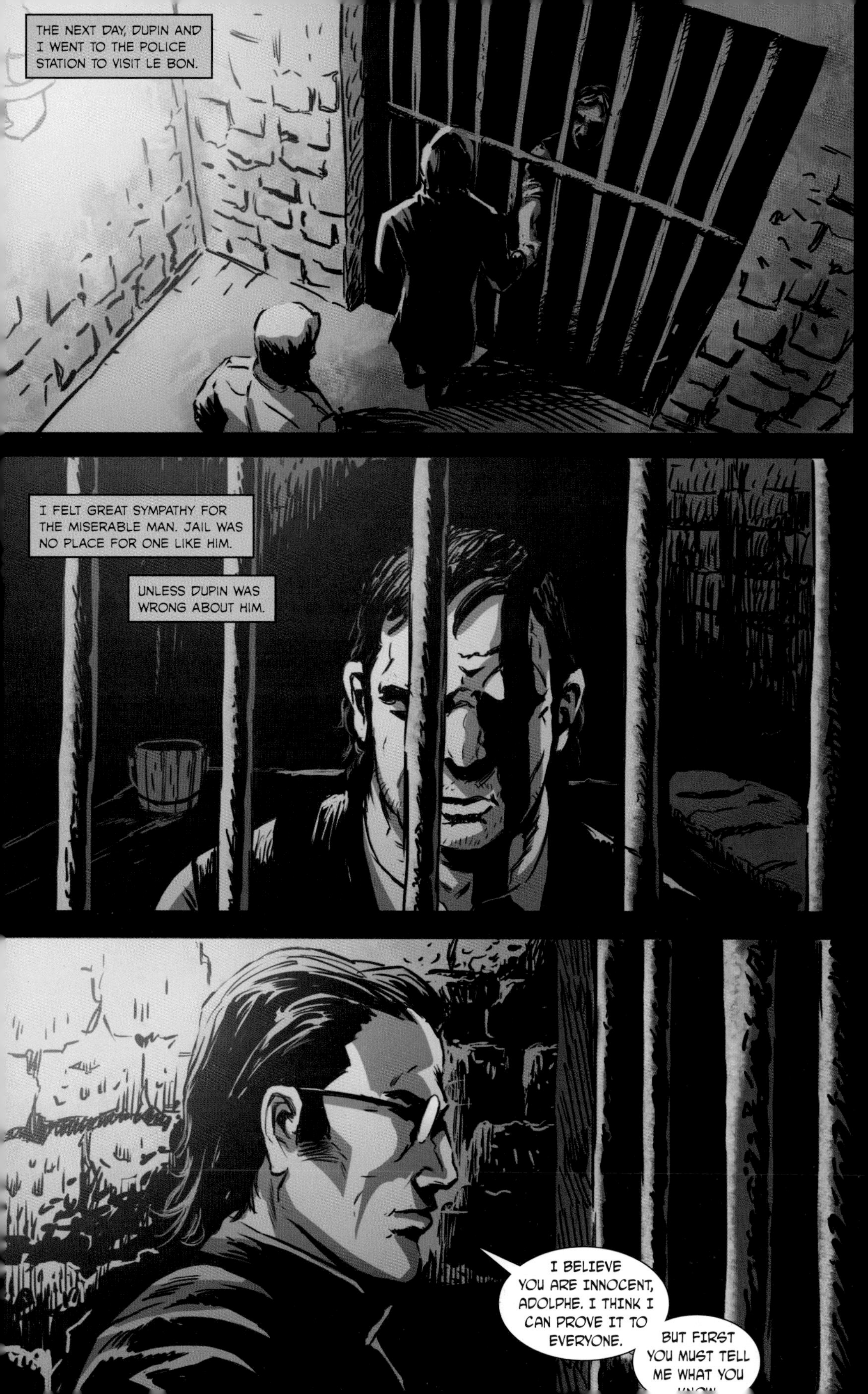
THE NEXT DAY, DUPIN AND I WENT TO THE POLICE STATION TO VISIT LE BON.
I FELT GREAT SYMPATHY FOR THE MISERABLE MAN. JAIL WAS NO PLACE FOR ONE LIKE HIM.
UNLESS DUPIN WAS WRONG ABOUT HIM.
I BELIEVE YOU ARE INNOCENT, ADOLPHE. I THINK I CAN PROVE IT TO EVERYONE.
BUT FIRST YOU MUST TELL ME WHAT YOU

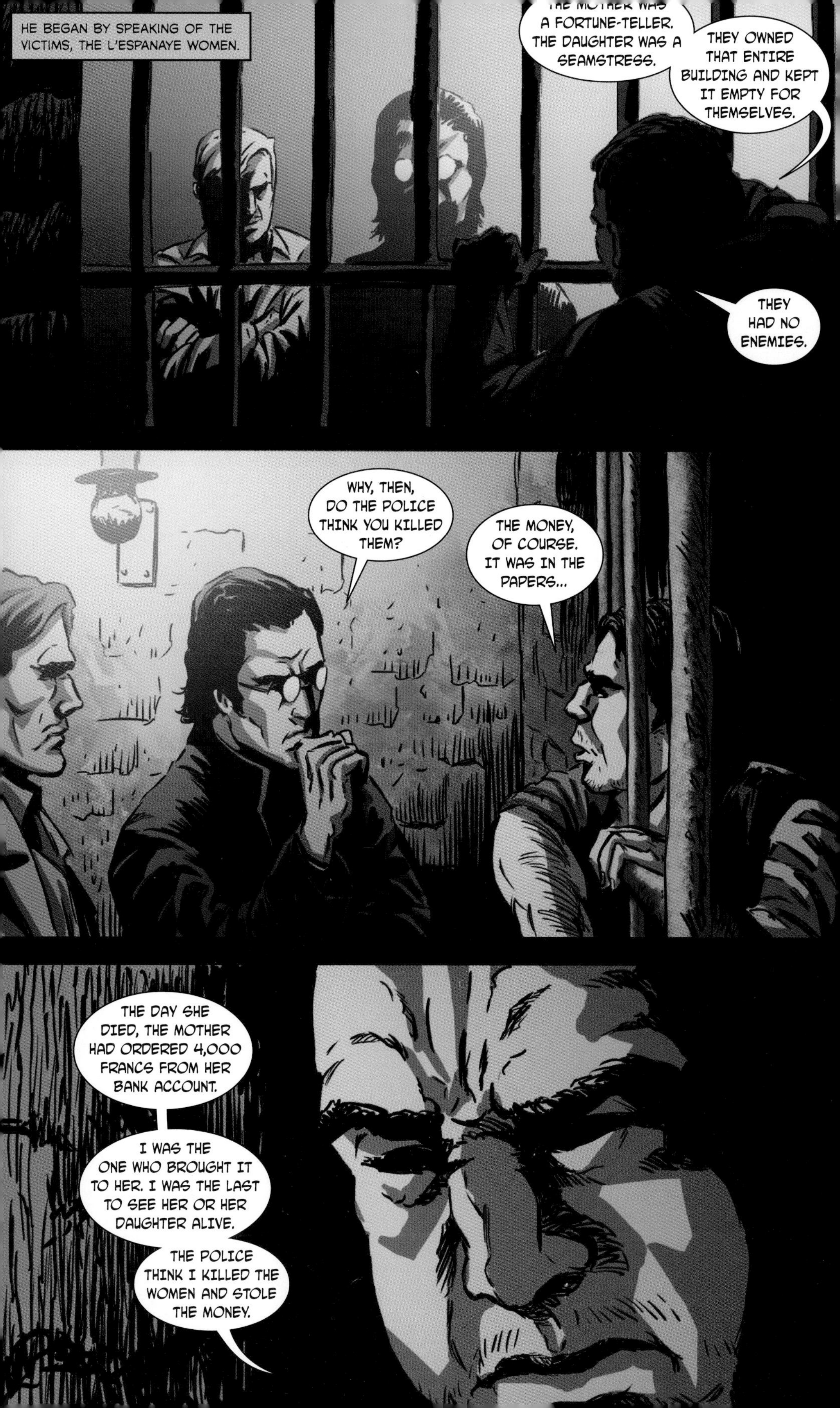
HE BEGAN BY SPEAKING OF THE VICTIMS, THE L'ESPANAYE WOMEN.
A FORTUNE-TELLER. THE DAUGHTER WAS A SEAMSTRESS.
THEY OWNED THAT ENTIRE BUILDING AND KEPT IT EMPTY FOR THEMSELVES.
THEY HAD NO ENEMIES.
WHY, THEN, DO THE POLICE THINK YOU KILLED THEM?
THE MONEY, OF COURSE. IT WAS IN THE PAPERS...
THE DAY SHE DIED, THE MOTHER HAD ORDERED 4,000 FRANCS FROM HER BANK ACCOUNT.
I WAS THE ONE WHO BROUGHT IT TO HER. I WAS THE LAST TO SEE HER OR HER DAUGHTER ALIVE.
THE POLICE THINK I KILLED THE WOMEN AND STOLE THE MONEY.

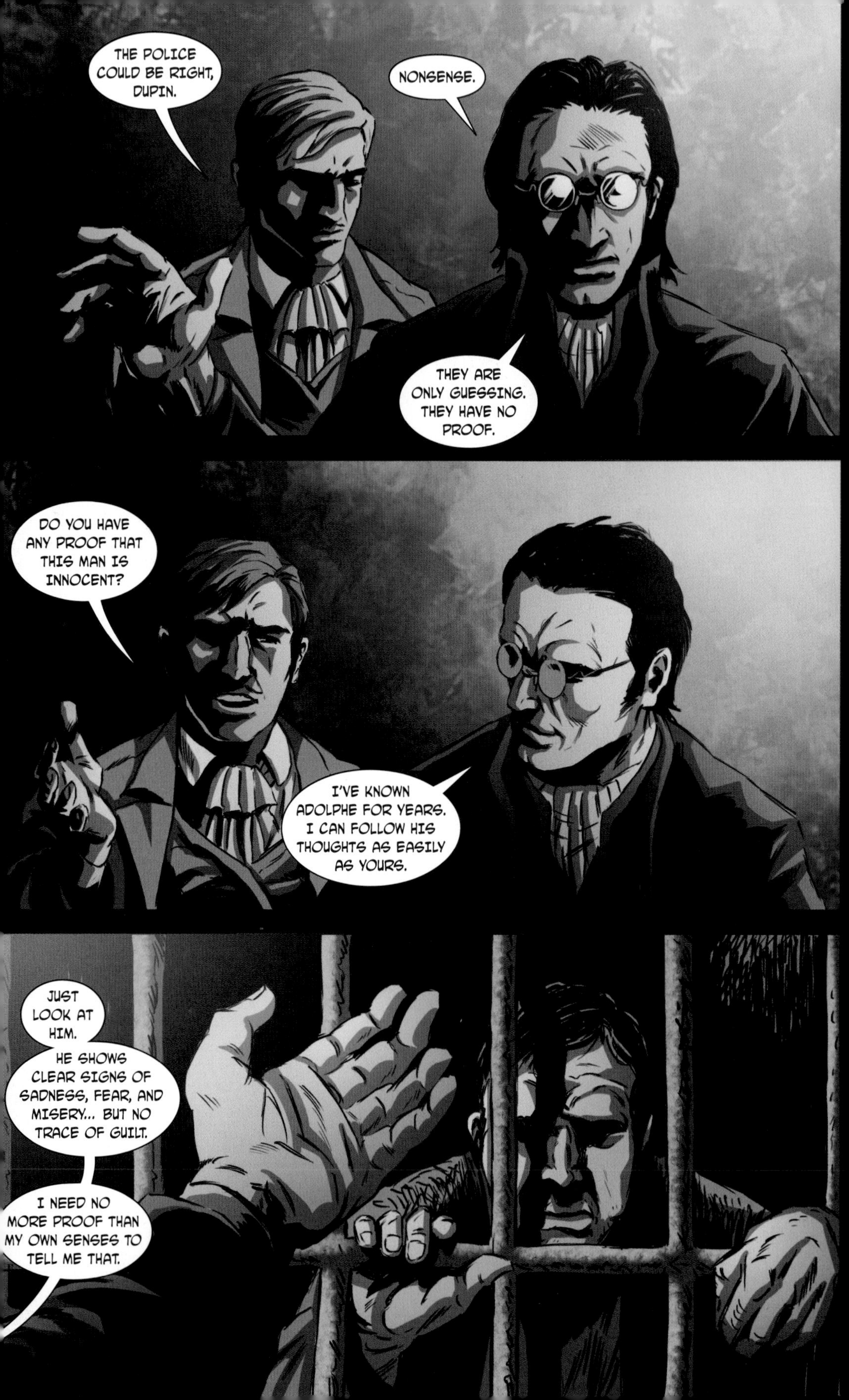
THE POLICE COULD BE RIGHT, DUPIN.
NONSENSE.
THEY ARE ONLY GUESSING. THEY HAVE NO PROOF.
DO YOU HAVE ANY PROOF THAT THIS MAN IS INNOCENT?
I'VE KNOWN ADOLPHE FOR YEARS. I CAN FOLLOW HIS THOUGHTS AS EASILY AS YOURS.
JUST LOOK AT HIM.
HE SHOWS CLEAR SIGNS OF SADNESS, FEAR, AND MISERY... BUT NO TRACE OF GUILT.
I NEED NO MORE PROOF THAN MY OWN SENSES TO TELL ME THAT.

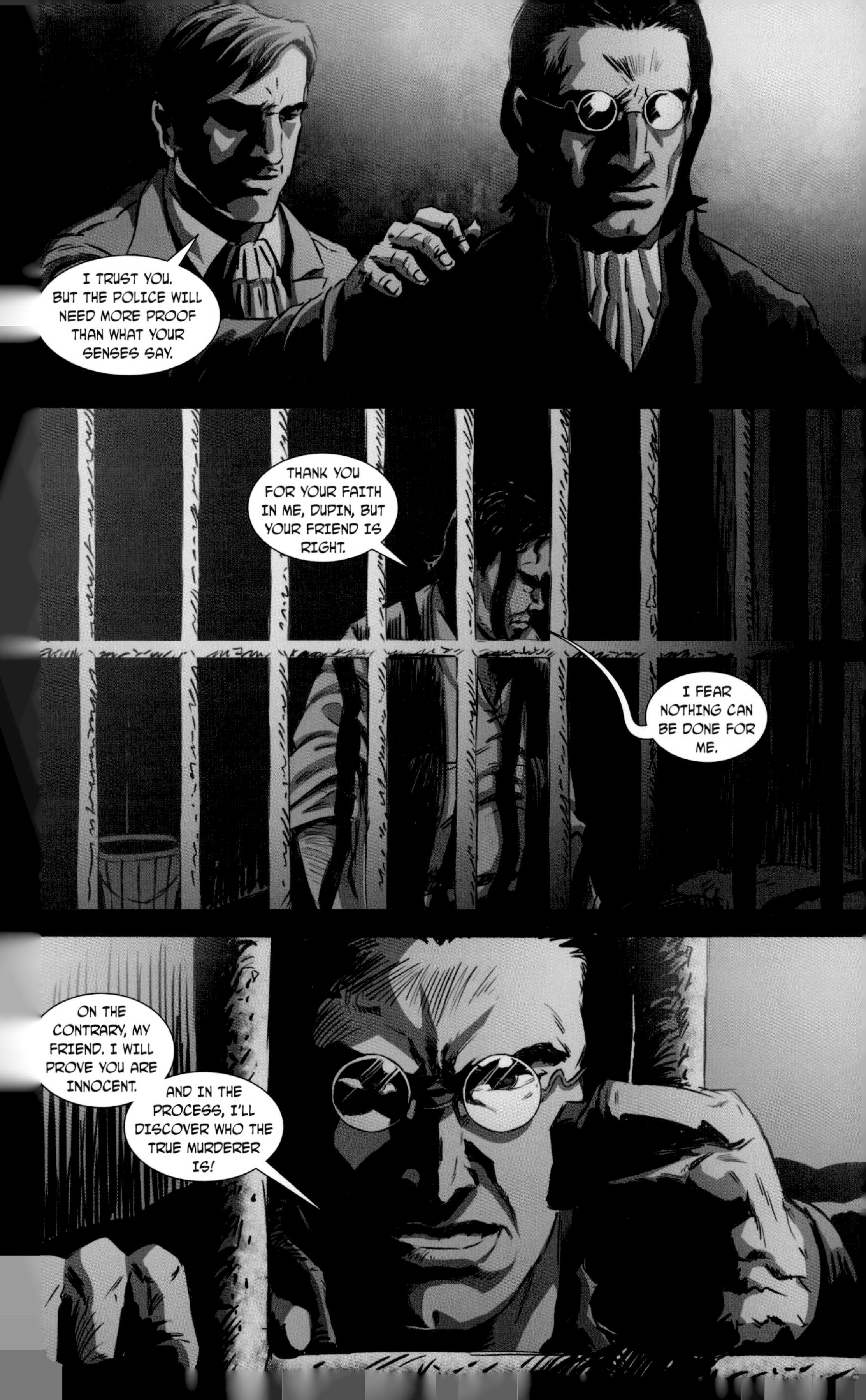
I TRUST YOU. BUT THE POLICE WILL NEED MORE PROOF THAN WHAT YOUR SENSES SAY.
THANK YOU FOR YOUR FAITH IN ME, DUPIN, BUT YOUR FRIEND IS RIGHT.
I FEAR NOTHING CAN BE DONE FOR ME.
ON THE CONTRARY, MY FRIEND. I WILL PROVE YOU ARE INNOCENT.
AND IN THE PROCESS, I'LL DISCOVER WHO THE TRUE MURDERER IS!

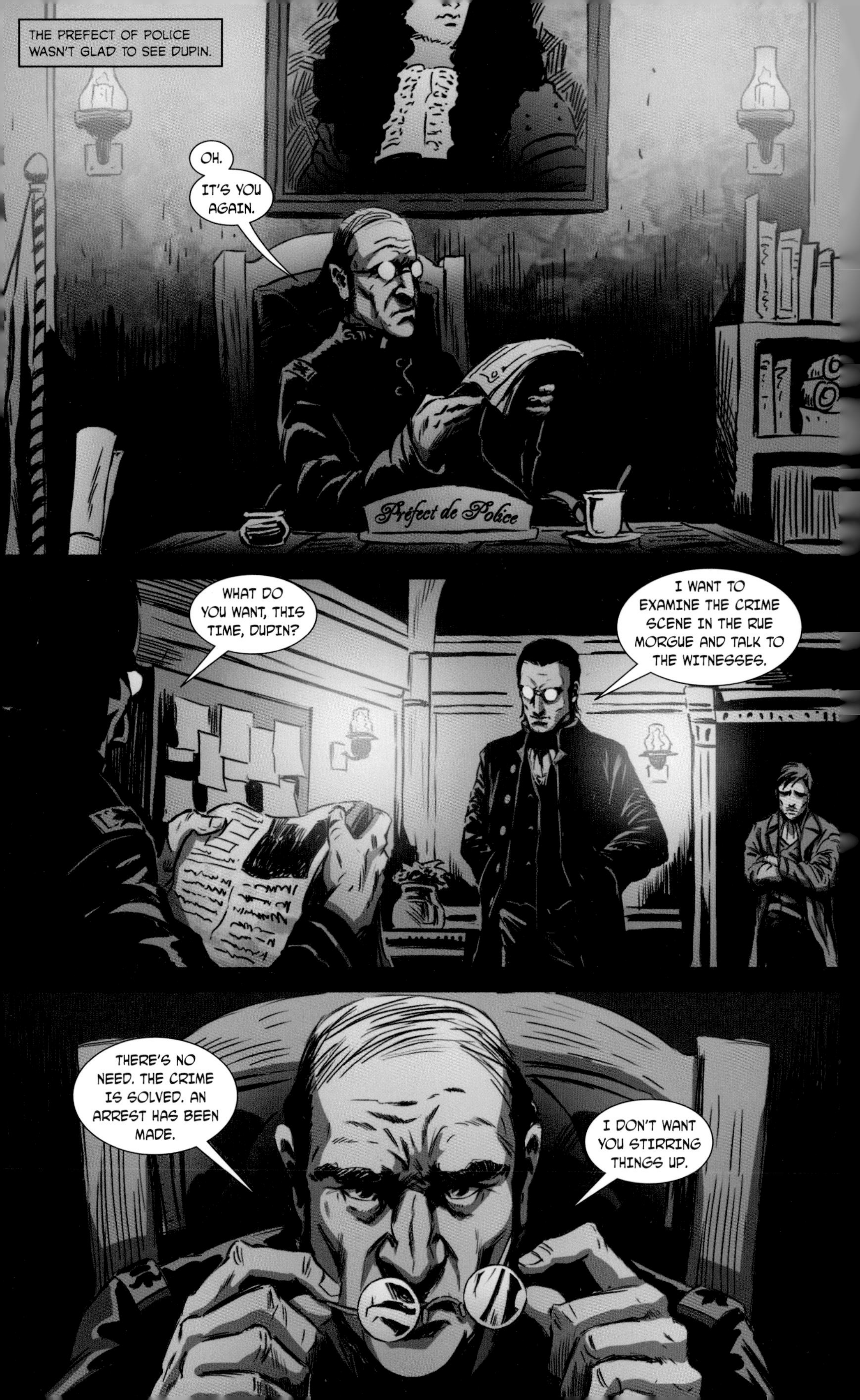
THE PREFECT OF POLICE WASN'T GLAD TO SEE DUPIN.
OH.
IT'S YOU AGAIN.
Préfect de Police
WHAT DO YOU WANT, THIS TIME, DUPIN?
I WANT TO EXAMINE THE CRIME SCENE IN THE RUE MORGUE AND TALK TO THE WITNESSES.
THERE'S NO NEED. THE CRIME IS SOLVED. AN ARREST HAS BEEN MADE.
I DON'T WANT YOU STIRRING THINGS UP.

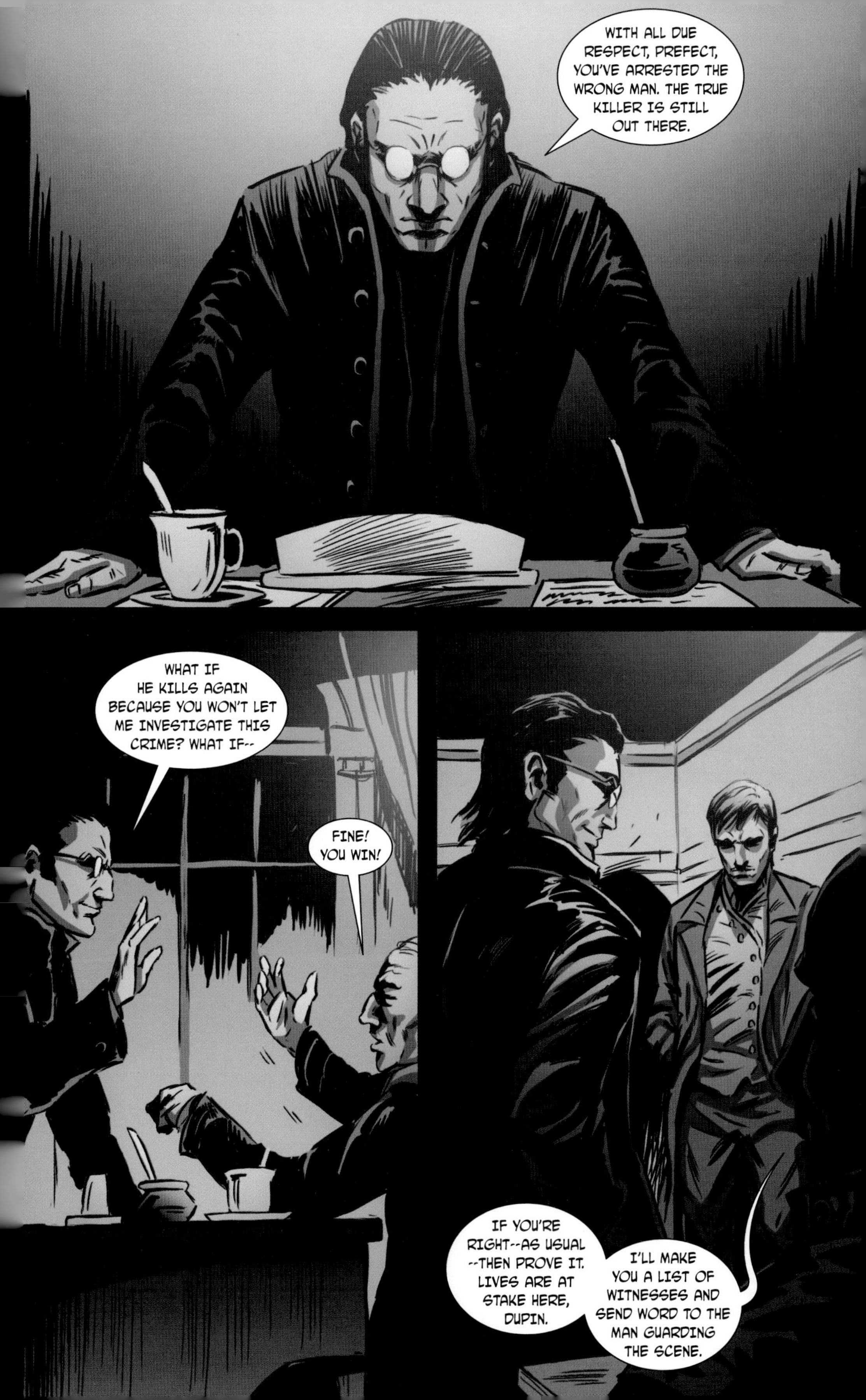
WITH ALL DUE RESPECT, PREFECT, YOU'VE ARRESTED THE WRONG MAN. THE TRUE KILLER IS STILL OUT THERE.
WHAT IF HE KILLS AGAIN BECAUSE YOU WON'T LET ME INVESTIGATE THIS CRIME? WHAT IF--
FINE! YOU WIN!
IF YOU'RE RIGHT--AS USUAL --THEN PROVE IT. LIVES ARE AT STAKE HERE, DUPIN.
I'LL MAKE YOU A LIST OF WITNESSES AND SEND WORD TO THE MAN GUARDING THE SCENE.

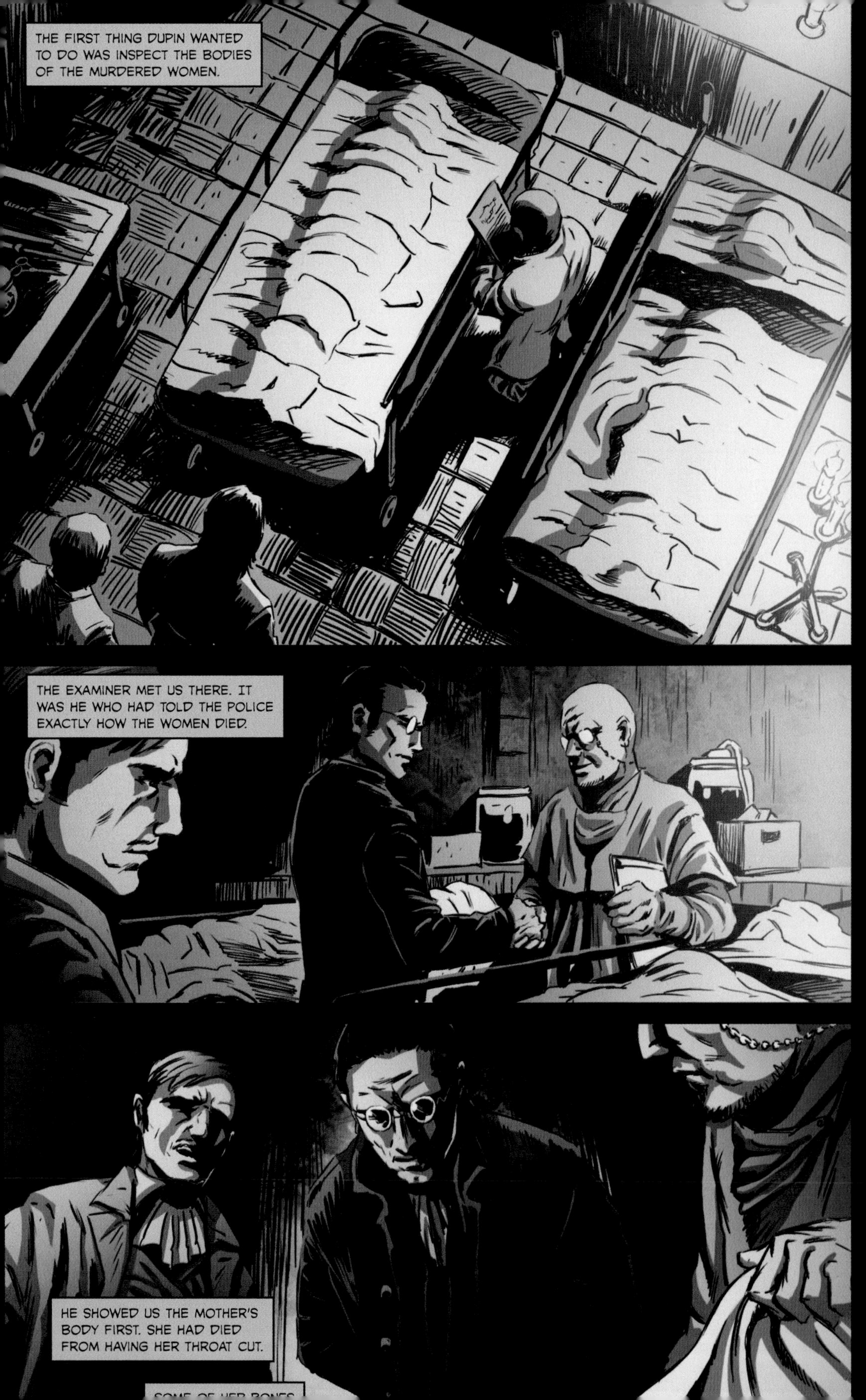
THE FIRST THING DUPIN WANTED TO DO WAS INSPECT THE BODIES OF THE MURDERED WOMEN.
THE EXAMINER MET US THERE. IT WAS HE WHO HAD TOLD THE POLICE EXACTLY HOW THE WOMEN DIED.
HE SHOWED US THE MOTHER'S BODY FIRST. SHE HAD DIED FROM HAVING HER THROAT CUT.

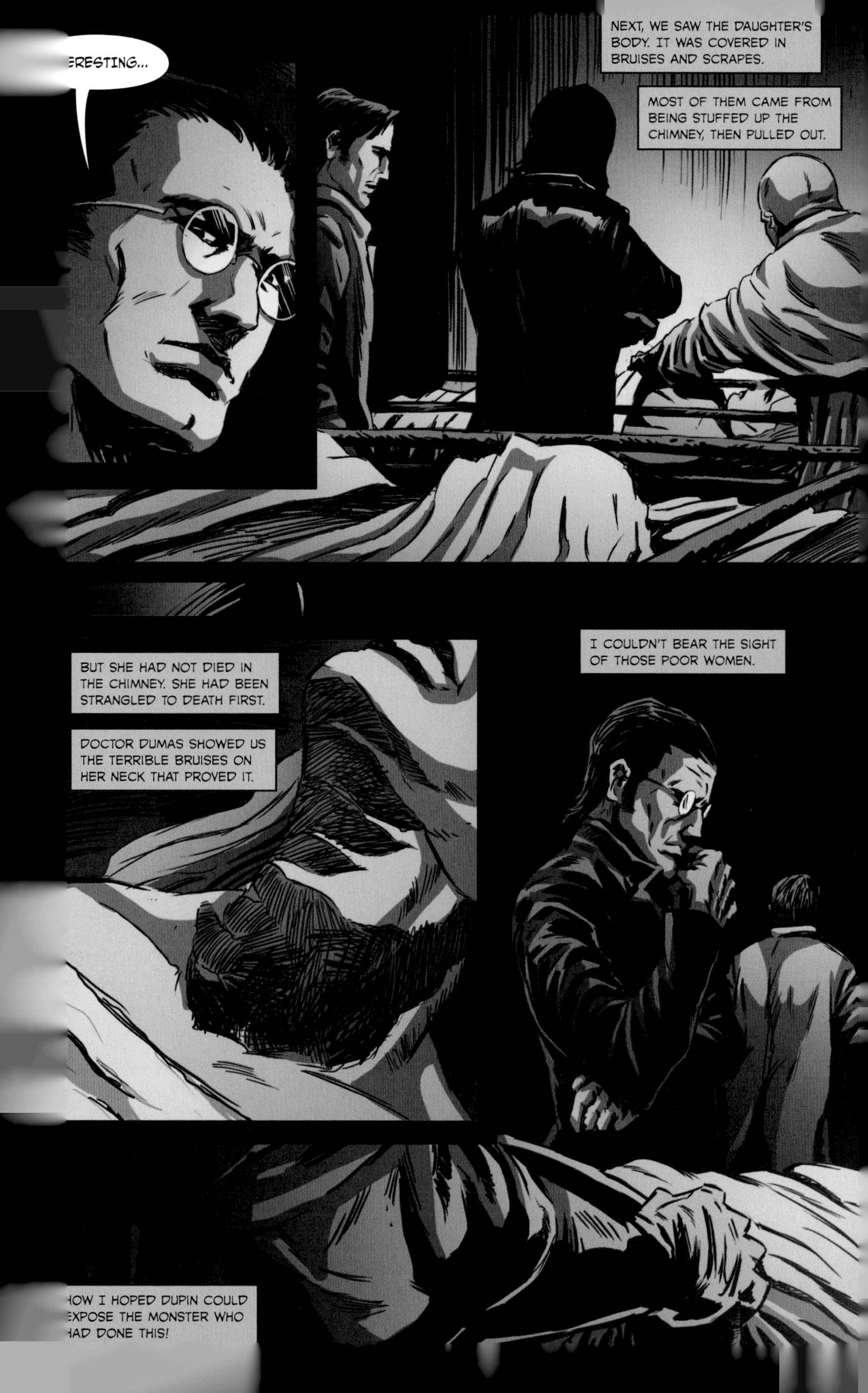

ERESTING...
NEXT, WE SAW THE DAUGHTER'S BODY. IT WAS COVERED IN BRUISES AND SCRAPES.
MOST OF THEM CAME FROM BEING STUFFED UP THE CHIMNEY, THEN PULLED OUT.
BUT SHE HAD NOT DIED IN THE CHIMNEY. SHE HAD BEEN STRANGLED TO DEATH FIRST.
DOCTOR DUMAS SHOWED US THE TERRIBLE BRUISES ON HER NECK THAT PROVED IT.
I COULDN'T BEAR THE SIGHT OF THOSE POOR WOMEN.
HOW I HOPED DUPIN COULD EXPOSE THE MONSTER WHO HAD DONE THIS!

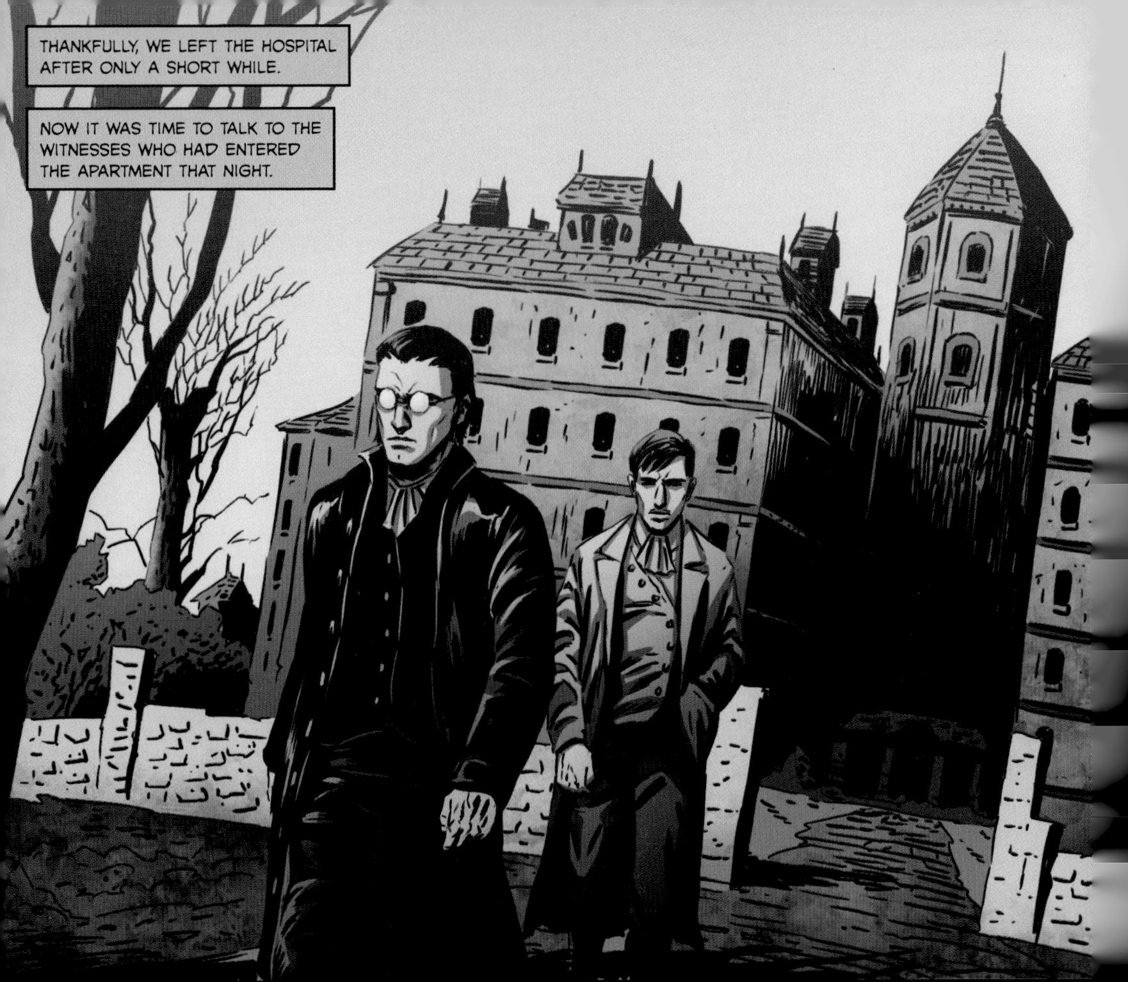
THANKFULLY, WE LEFT THE HOSPITAL AFTER ONLY A SHORT WHILE.
NOW IT WAS TIME TO TALK TO THE WITNESSES WHO HAD ENTERED THE APARTMENT THAT NIGHT.

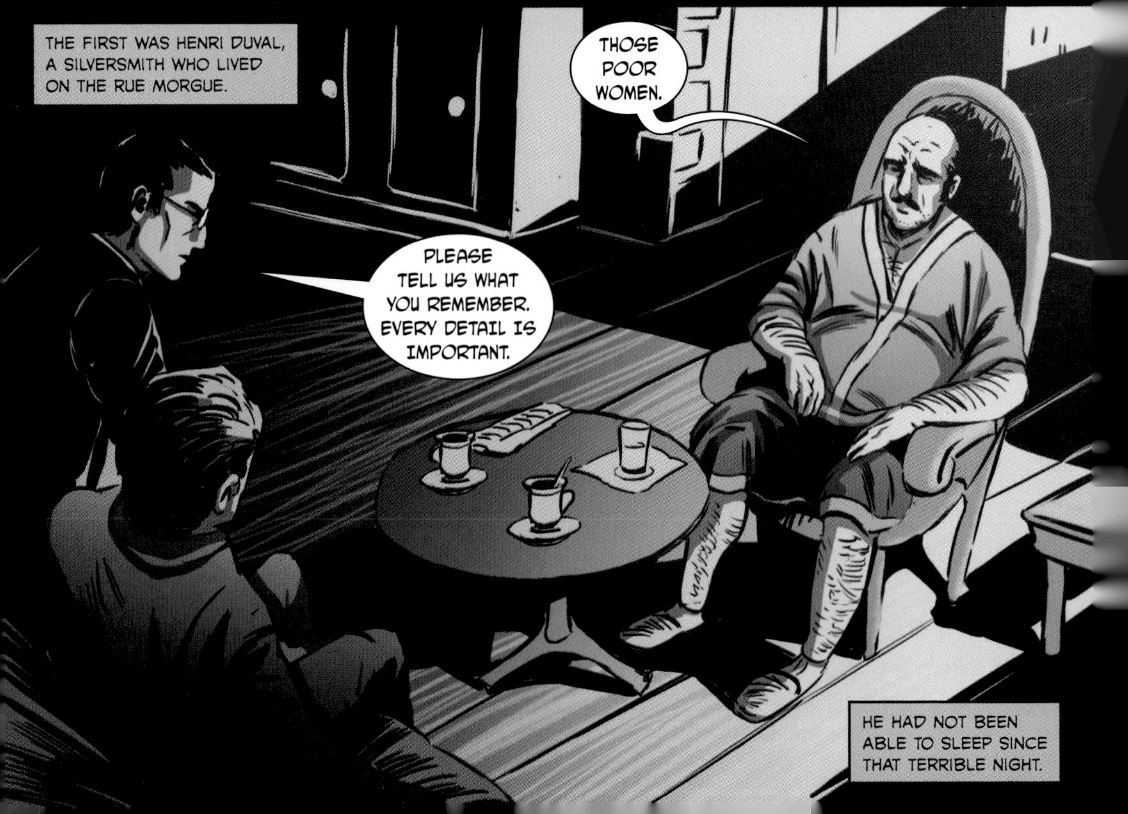
THE FIRST WAS HENRI DUVAL, A SILVERSMITH WHO LIVED ON THE RUE MORGUE.
THOSE POOR WOMEN.
PLEASE TELL US WHAT YOU REMEMBER. EVERY DETAIL IS IMPORTANT.
HE HAD NOT BEEN ABLE TO SLEEP SINCE THAT TERRIBLE NIGHT.

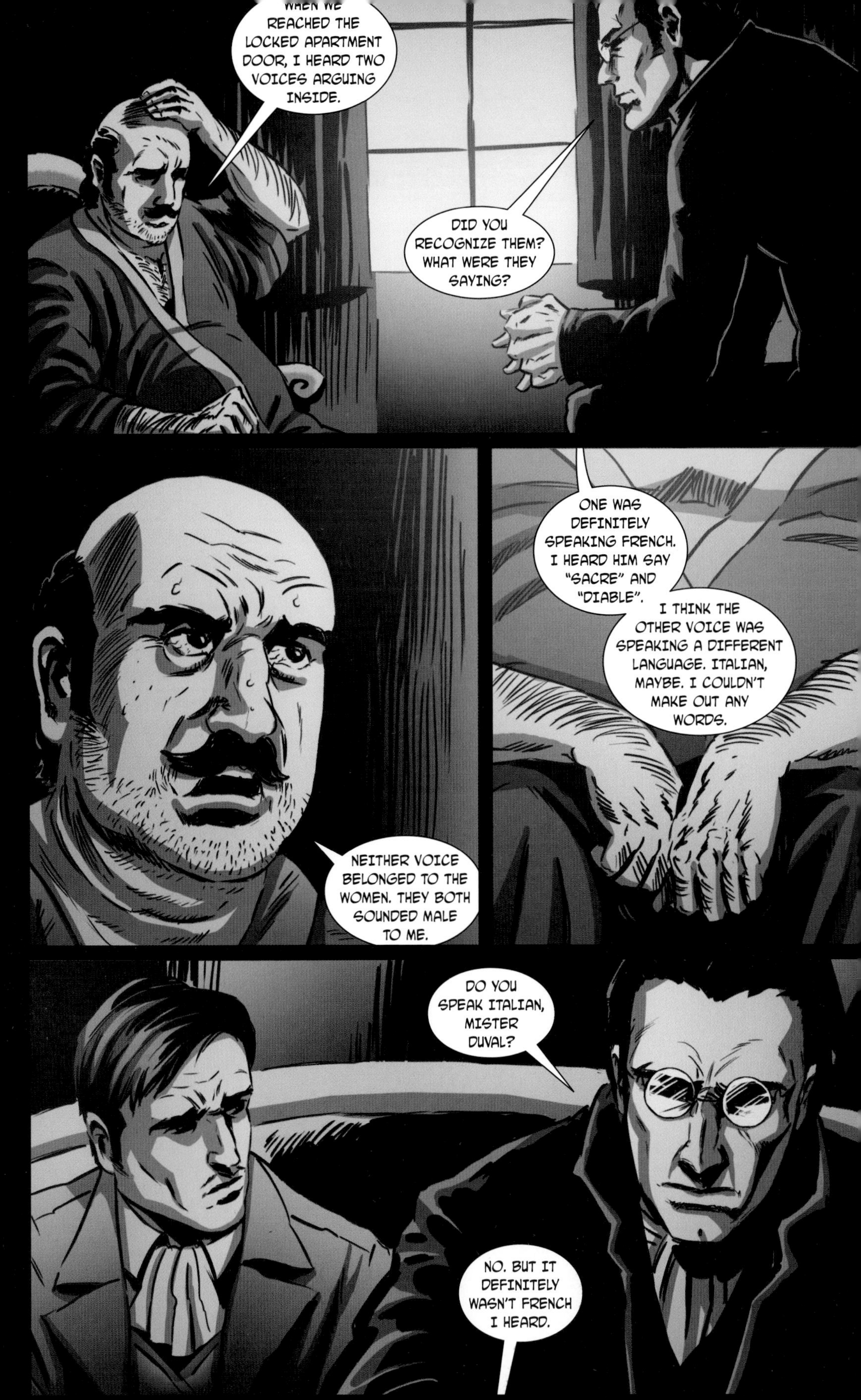
WHEN WE REACHED THE LOCKED APARTMENT DOOR, I HEARD TWO VOICES ARGUING INSIDE.
DID YOU RECOGNIZE THEM? WHAT WERE THEY SAYING?
NEITHER VOICE BELONGED TO THE WOMEN. THEY BOTH SOUNDED MALE TO ME.
ONE WAS DEFINITELY SPEAKING FRENCH. I HEARD HIM SAY "SACRE" AND "DIABLE".
I THINK THE OTHER VOICE WAS SPEAKING A DIFFERENT LANGUAGE. ITALIAN, MAYBE. I COULDN'T MAKE OUT ANY WORDS.
DO YOU SPEAK ITALIAN, MISTER DUVAL?
NO. BUT IT DEFINITELY WASN'T FRENCH I HEARD.

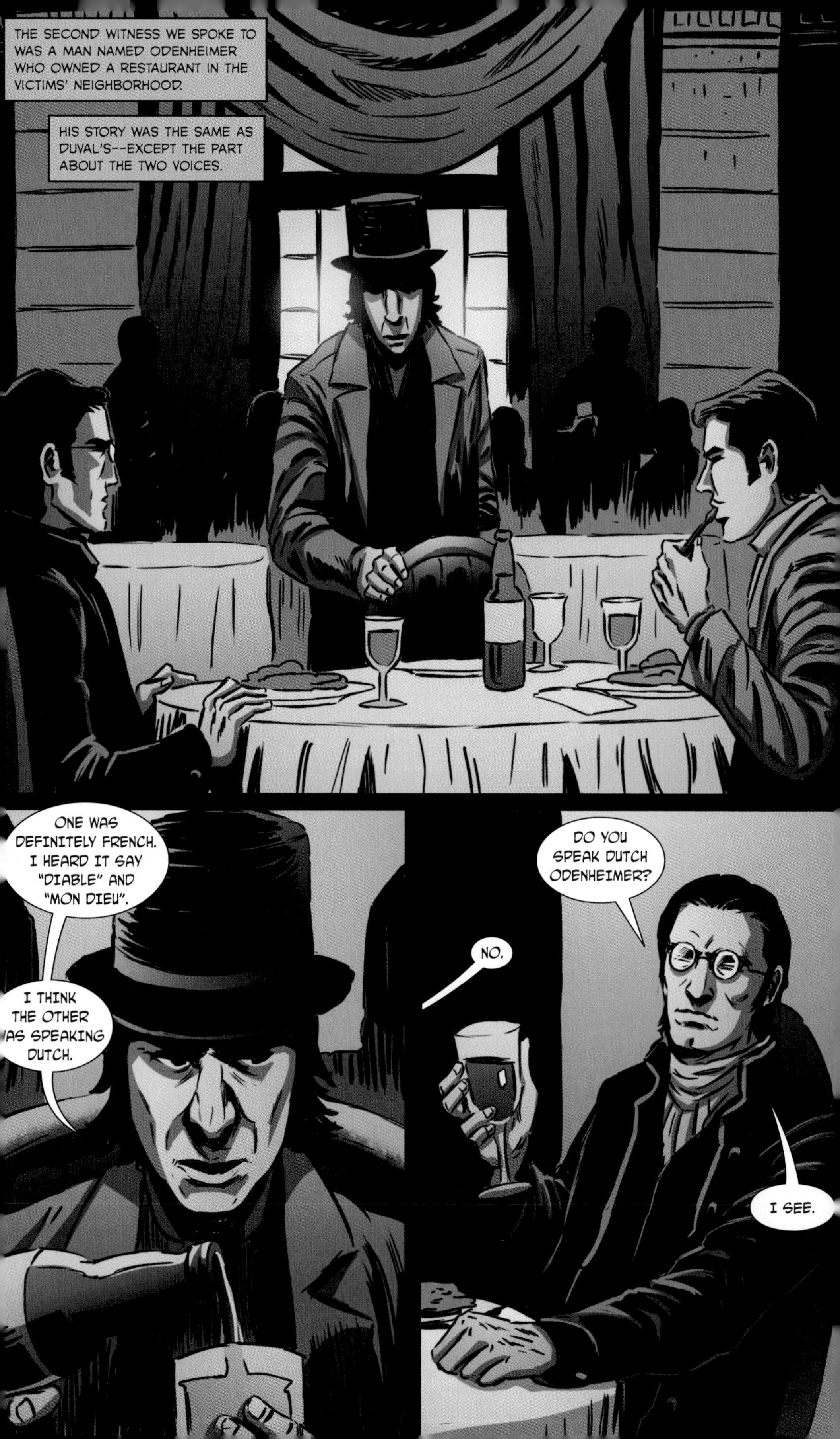
THE SECOND WITNESS WE SPOKE TO WAS A MAN NAMED ODENHEIMER WHO OWNED A RESTAURANT IN THE VICTIMS' NEIGHBORHOOD.
HIS STORY WAS THE SAME AS DUVAL'S--EXCEPT THE PART ABOUT THE TWO VOICES.
ONE WAS DEFINITELY FRENCH. I HEARD IT SAY "DIABLE" AND "MON DIEU".
I THINK THE OTHER WAS SPEAKING DUTCH.
DO YOU SPEAK DUTCH ODENHEIMER?
NO.
I SEE.

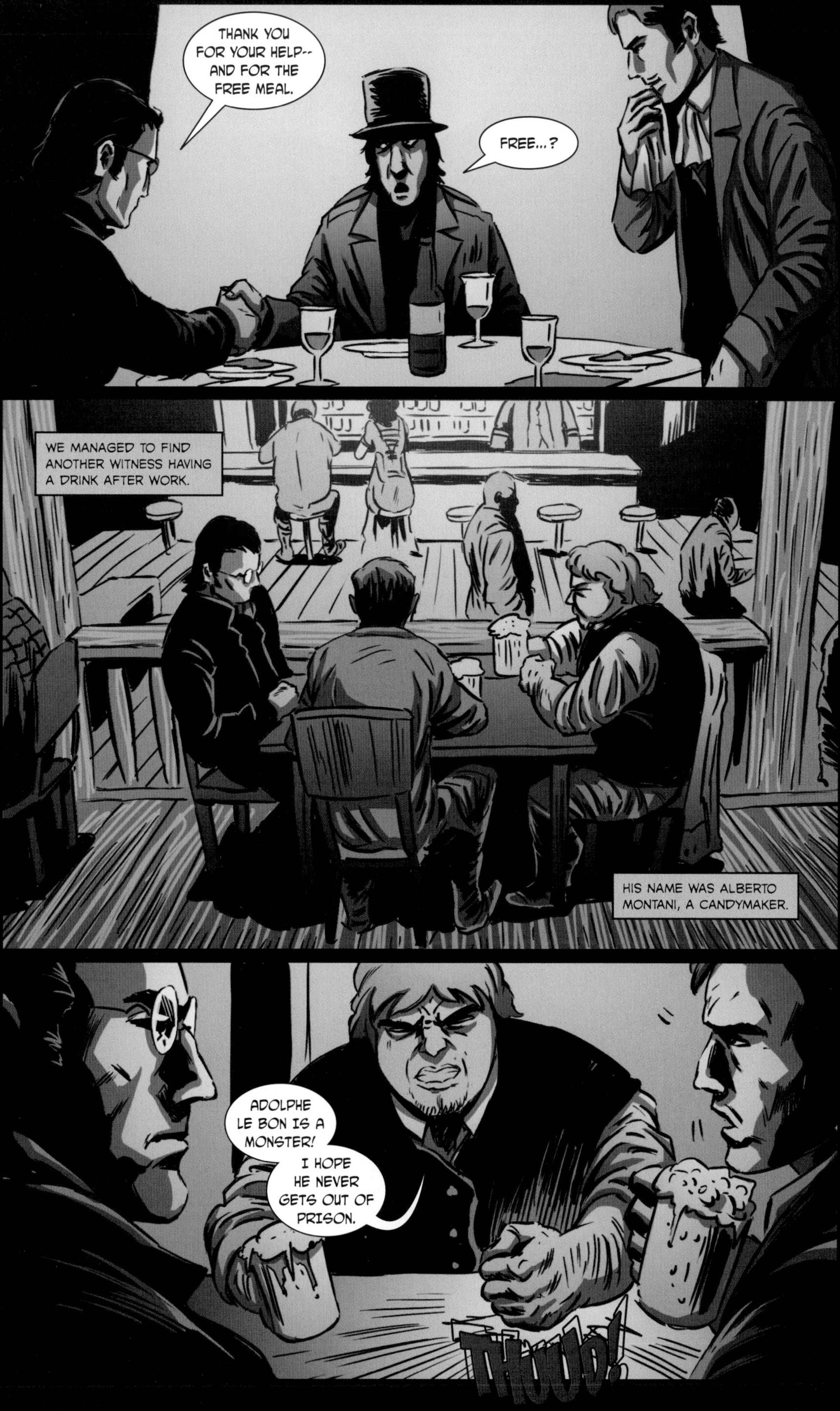
THANK YOU FOR YOUR HELP-- AND FOR THE FREE MEAL.
FREE...?
WE MANAGED TO FIND ANOTHER WITNESS HAVING A DRINK AFTER WORK.
HIS NAME WAS ALBERTO MONTANI, A CANDYMAKER.
ADOLPHE LE BON IS A MONSTER!
I HOPE HE NEVER GETS OUT OF PRISON.
THUD!

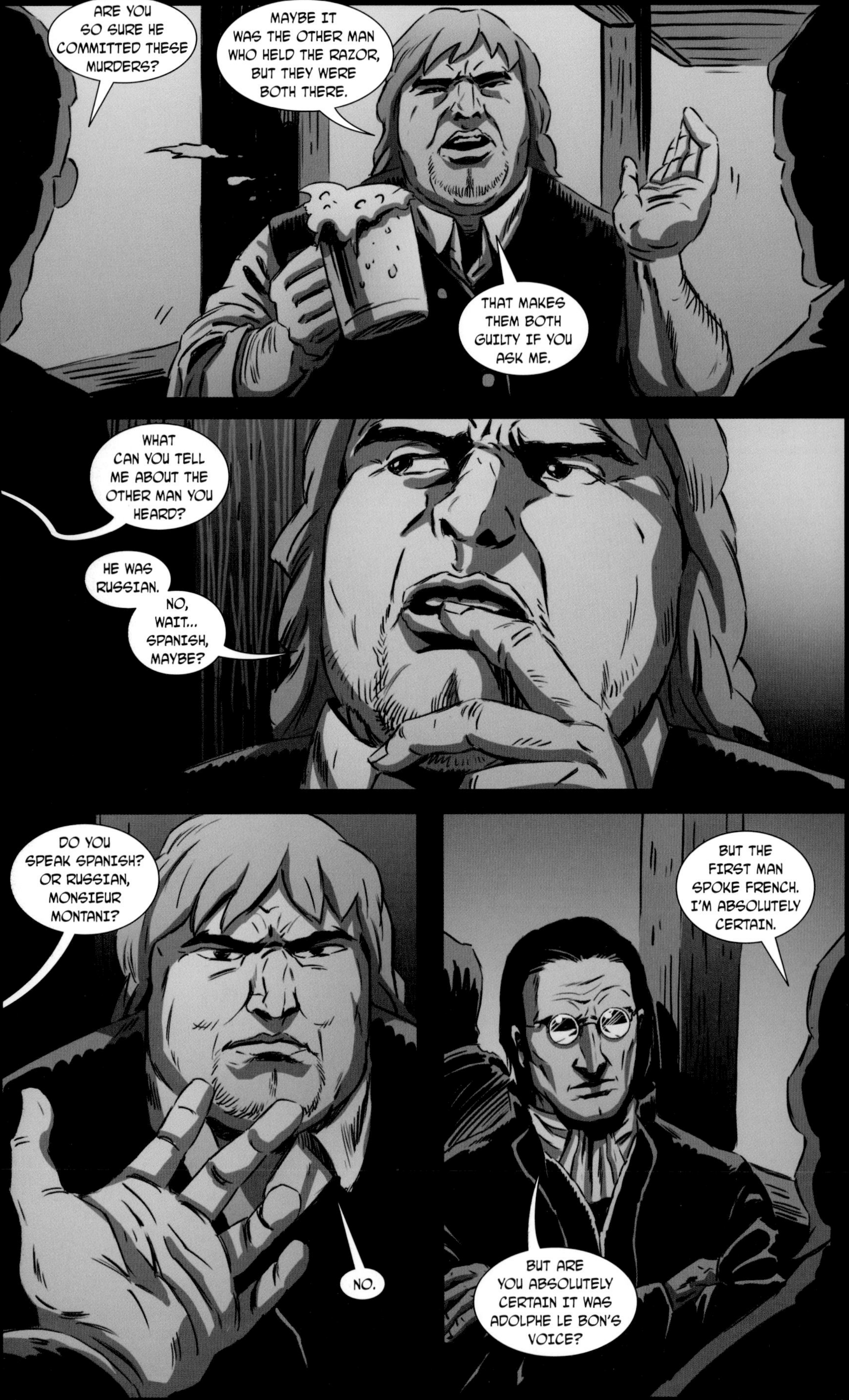
ARE YOU SO SURE HE COMMITTED THESE MURDERS?
MAYBE IT WAS THE OTHER MAN WHO HELD THE RAZOR, BUT THEY WERE BOTH THERE.
THAT MAKES THEM BOTH GUILTY IF YOU ASK ME.
WHAT CAN YOU TELL ME ABOUT THE OTHER MAN YOU HEARD?
HE WAS RUSSIAN.
NO, WAIT... SPANISH, MAYBE?
DO YOU SPEAK SPANISH? OR RUSSIAN, MONSIEUR MONTANI?
NO.
BUT THE FIRST MAN SPOKE FRENCH. I'M ABSOLUTELY CERTAIN.
BUT ARE YOU ABSOLUTELY CERTAIN IT WAS ADOLPHE LE BON'S VOICE?

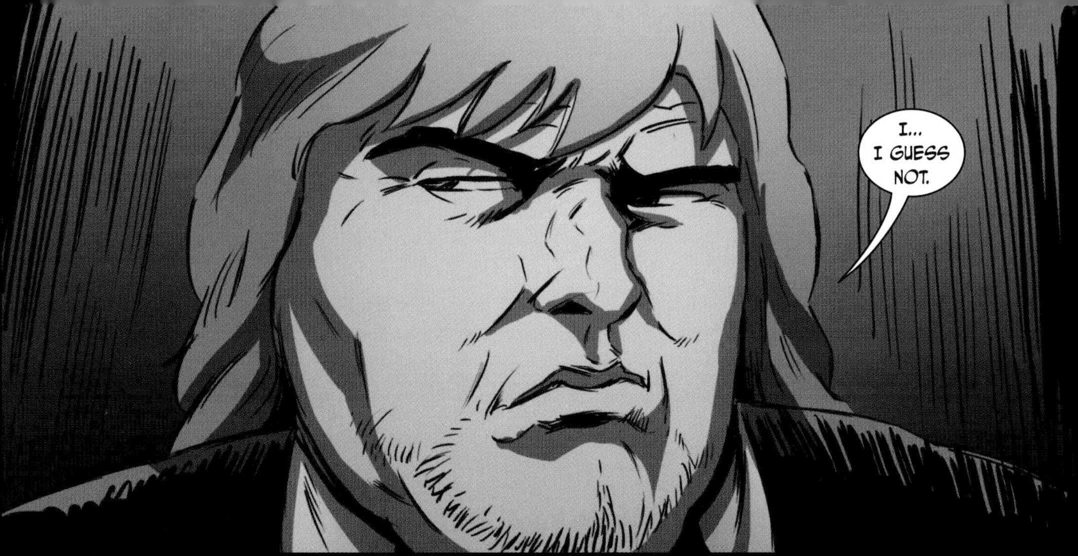
I...
I GUESS
NOT.

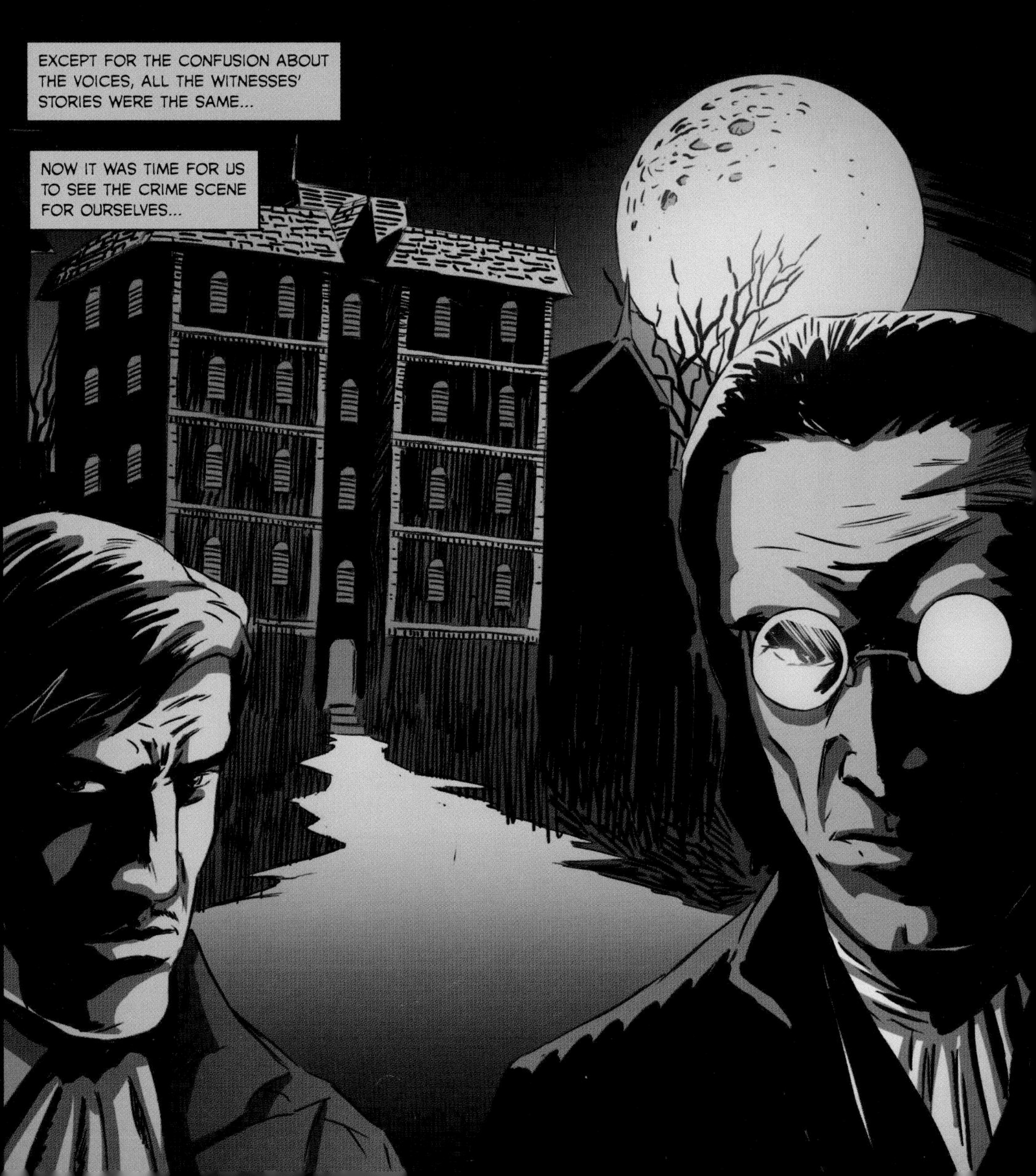
EXCEPT FOR THE CONFUSION ABOUT
THE VOICES, ALL THE WITNESSES'
STORIES WERE THE SAME...
NOW IT WAS TIME FOR US
TO SEE THE CRIME SCENE
FOR OURSELVES...

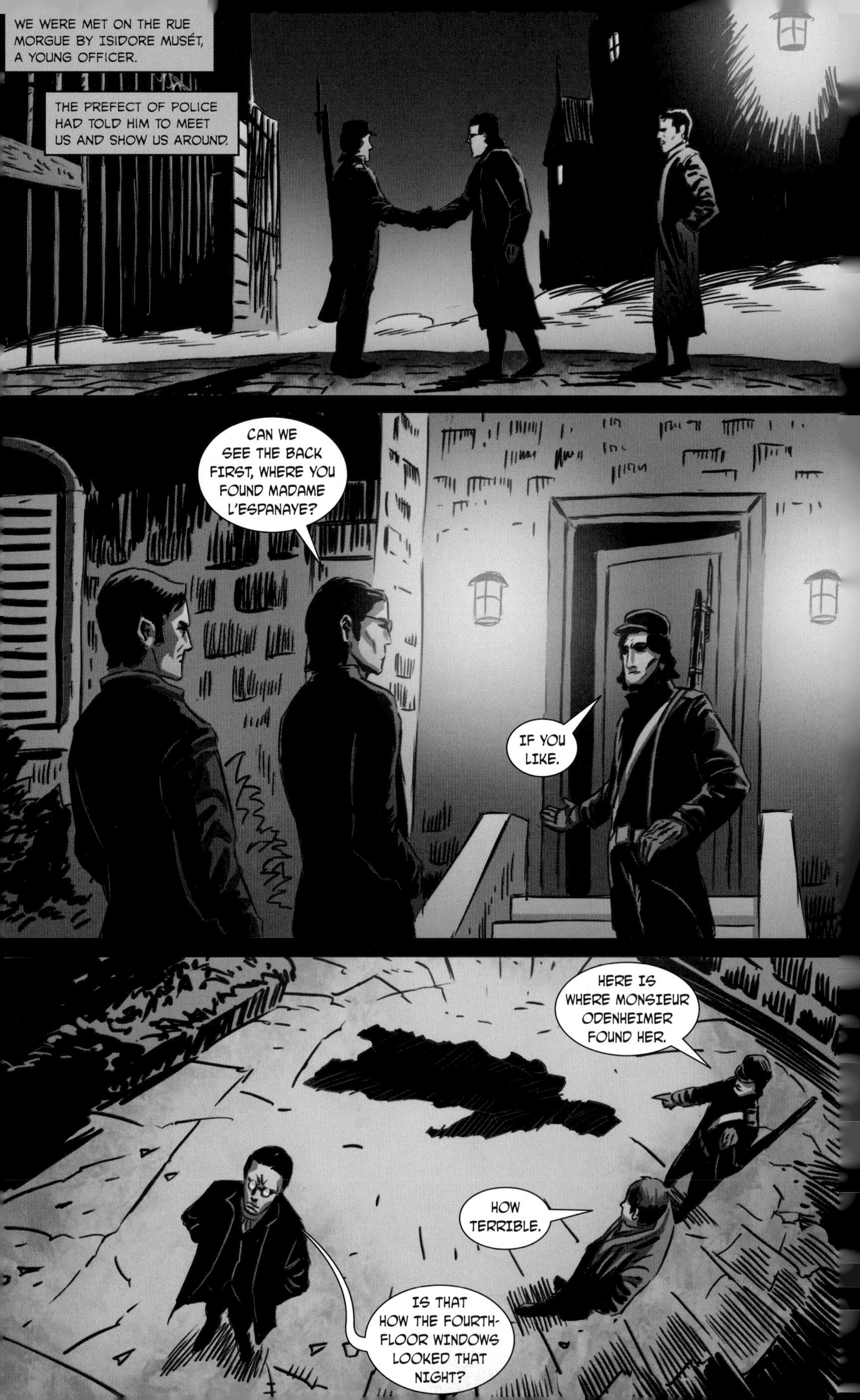
WE WERE MET ON THE RUE MORGUE BY ISIDORE MUSÉT, A YOUNG OFFICER.
THE PREFECT OF POLICE HAD TOLD HIM TO MEET US AND SHOW US AROUND.
CAN WE SEE THE BACK FIRST, WHERE YOU FOUND MADAME L'ESPANAYE?
IF YOU LIKE.
HERE IS WHERE MONSIEUR ODENHEIMER FOUND HER.
HOW TERRIBLE.
IS THAT HOW THE FOURTH-FLOOR WINDOWS LOOKED THAT NIGHT?

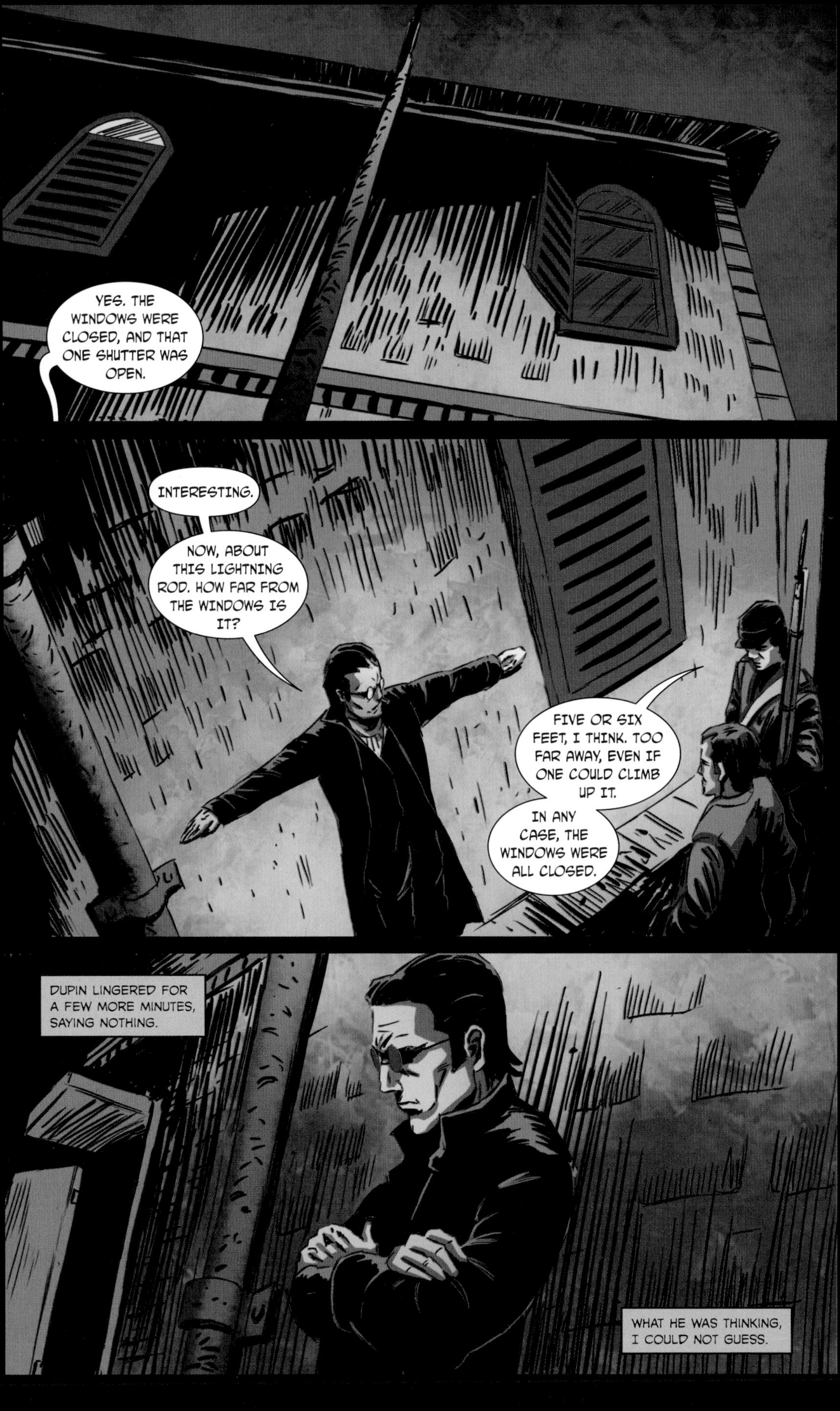
YES. THE WINDOWS WERE CLOSED, AND THAT ONE SHUTTER WAS OPEN.
INTERESTING.
NOW, ABOUT THIS LIGHTNING ROD. HOW FAR FROM THE WINDOWS IS IT?
FIVE OR SIX FEET, I THINK. TOO FAR AWAY, EVEN IF ONE COULD CLIMB UP IT.
IN ANY CASE, THE WINDOWS WERE ALL CLOSED.
DUPIN LINGERED FOR A FEW MORE MINUTES, SAYING NOTHING.
WHAT HE WAS THINKING, I COULD NOT GUESS.

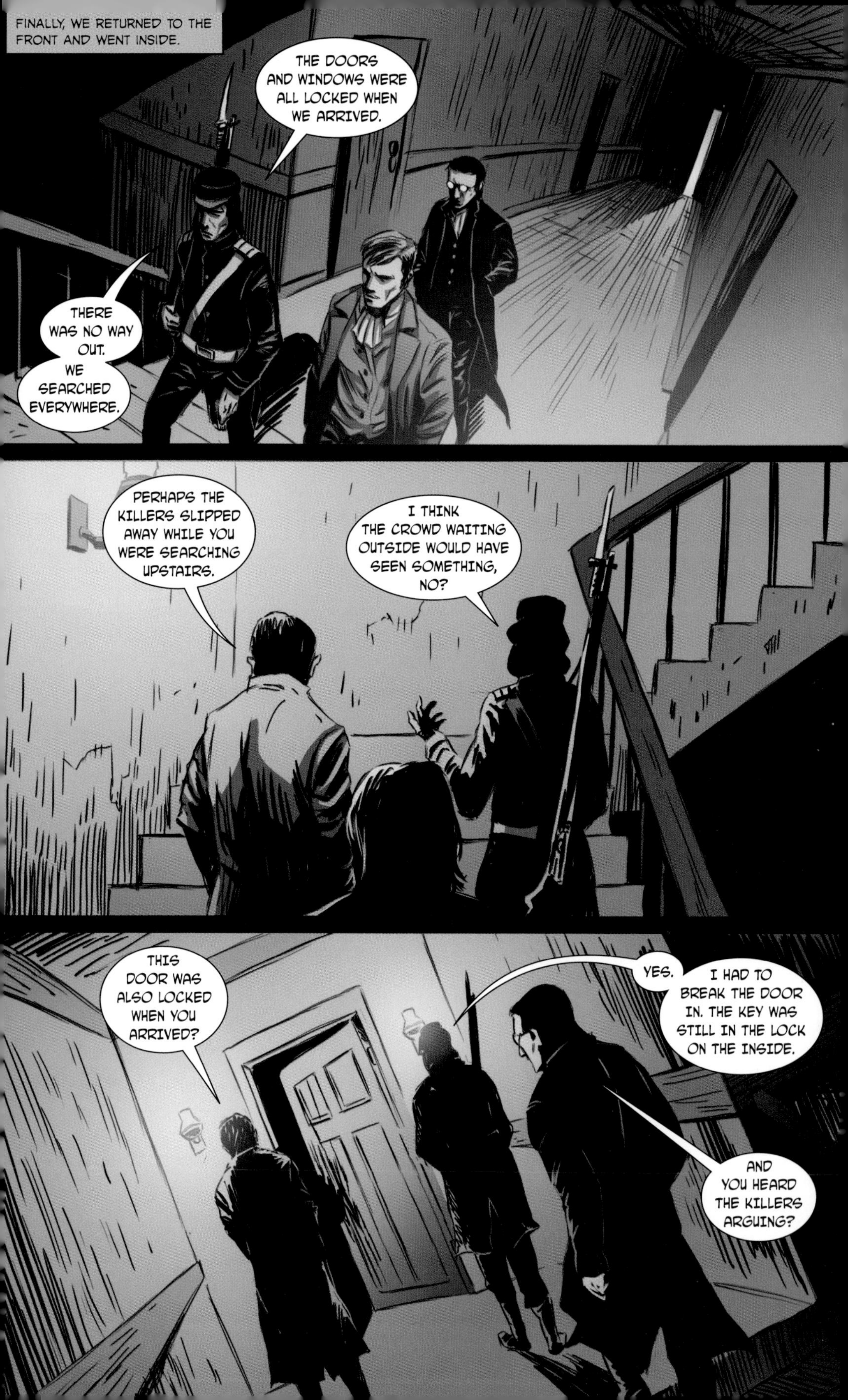
FINALLY, WE RETURNED TO THE FRONT AND WENT INSIDE.
THE DOORS AND WINDOWS WERE ALL LOCKED WHEN WE ARRIVED.
THERE WAS NO WAY OUT.
WE SEARCHED EVERYWHERE.
PERHAPS THE KILLERS SLIPPED AWAY WHILE YOU WERE SEARCHING UPSTAIRS.
I THINK THE CROWD WAITING OUTSIDE WOULD HAVE SEEN SOMETHING, NO?
THIS DOOR WAS ALSO LOCKED WHEN YOU ARRIVED?
YES.
I HAD TO BREAK THE DOOR IN. THE KEY WAS STILL IN THE LOCK ON THE INSIDE.
AND YOU HEARD THE KILLERS ARGUING?

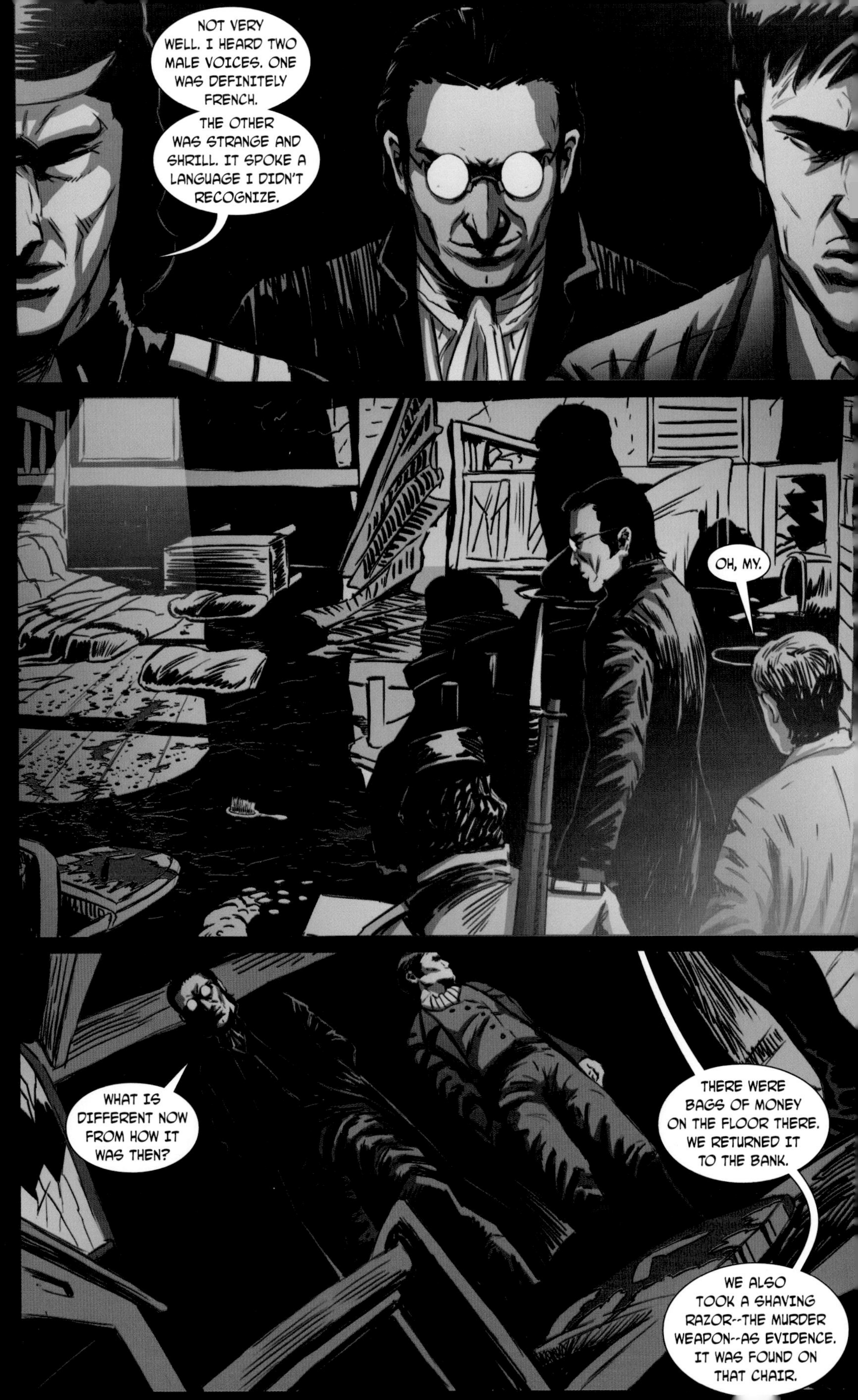
NOT VERY WELL. I HEARD TWO MALE VOICES. ONE WAS DEFINITELY FRENCH.
THE OTHER WAS STRANGE AND SHRILL. IT SPOKE A LANGUAGE I DIDN'T RECOGNIZE.
OH, MY.
WHAT IS DIFFERENT NOW FROM HOW IT WAS THEN?
THERE WERE BAGS OF MONEY ON THE FLOOR THERE. WE RETURNED IT TO THE BANK.
WE ALSO TOOK A SHAVING RAZOR--THE MURDER WEAPON--AS EVIDENCE. IT WAS FOUND ON THAT CHAIR.

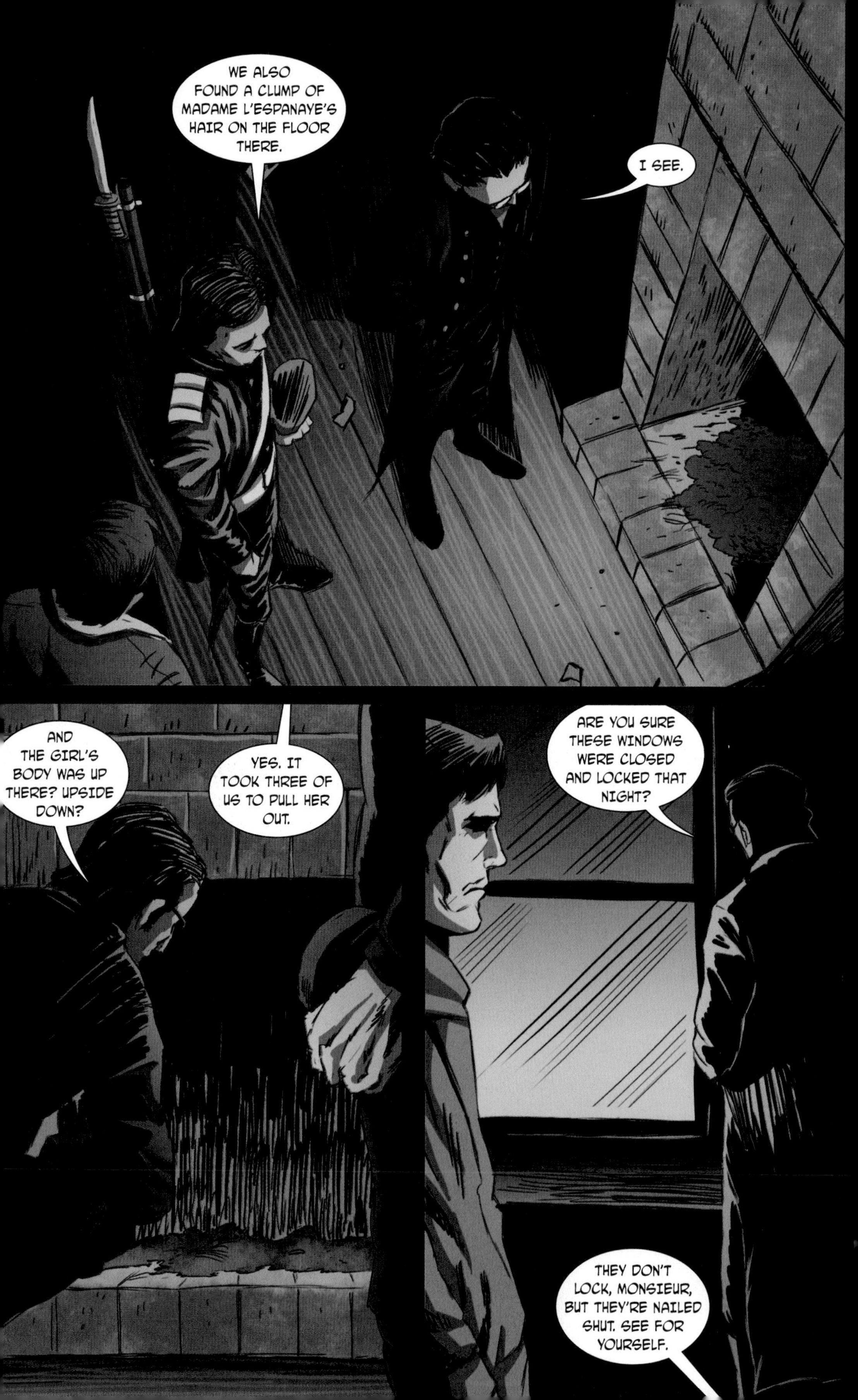
WE ALSO FOUND A CLUMP OF MADAME L'ESPANAYE'S HAIR ON THE FLOOR THERE.
I SEE.
AND THE GIRL'S BODY WAS UP THERE? UPSIDE DOWN?
YES. IT TOOK THREE OF US TO PULL HER OUT.
ARE YOU SURE THESE WINDOWS WERE CLOSED AND LOCKED THAT NIGHT?
THEY DON'T LOCK, MONSIEUR, BUT THEY'RE NAILED SHUT. SEE FOR YOURSELF.

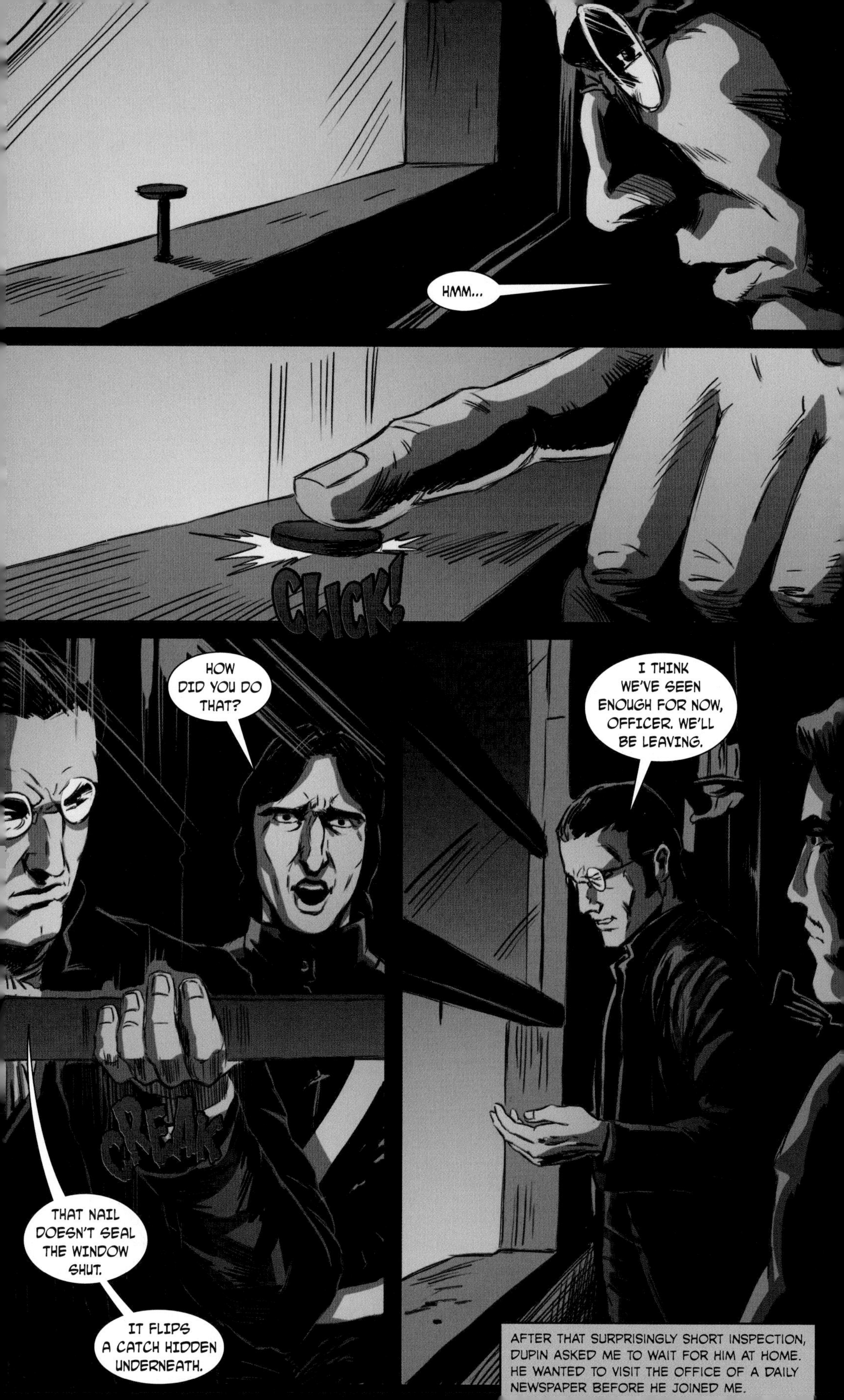
HMM...
CLICK!
HOW DID YOU DO THAT?
CREAK
THAT NAIL DOESN'T SEAL THE WINDOW SHUT.
IT FLIPS A CATCH HIDDEN UNDERNEATH.
I THINK WE'VE SEEN ENOUGH FOR NOW, OFFICER. WE'LL BE LEAVING.
AFTER THAT SURPRISINGLY SHORT INSPECTION, DUPIN ASKED ME TO WAIT FOR HIM AT HOME. HE WANTED TO VISIT THE OFFICE OF A DAILY NEWSPAPER BEFORE HE JOINED ME.

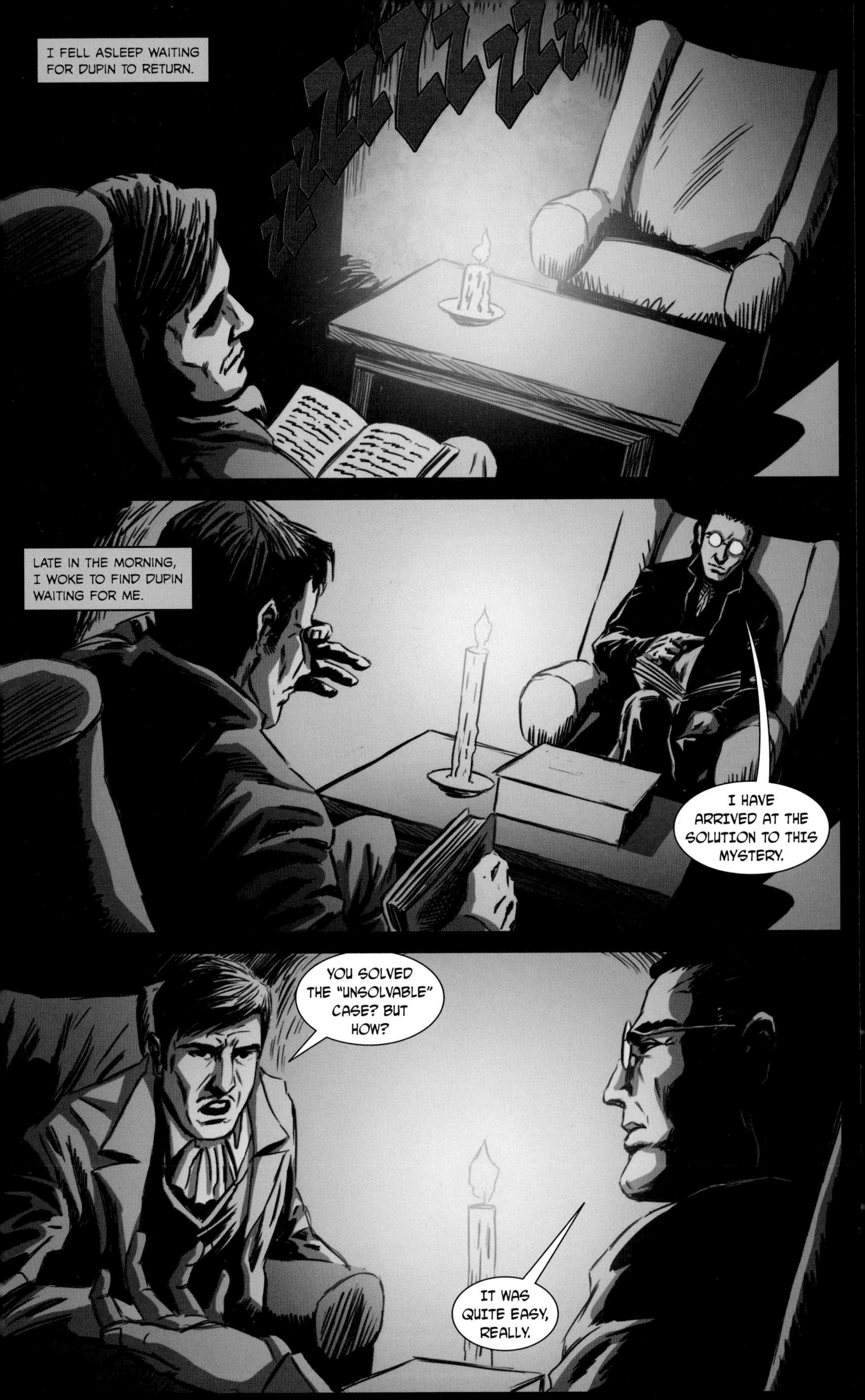
I FELL ASLEEP WAITING FOR DUPIN TO RETURN.
ZZZZZZZzzz
LATE IN THE MORNING, I WOKE TO FIND DUPIN WAITING FOR ME.
I HAVE ARRIVED AT THE SOLUTION TO THIS MYSTERY.
YOU SOLVED THE "UNSOLVABLE" CASE? BUT HOW?
IT WAS QUITE EASY, REALLY.

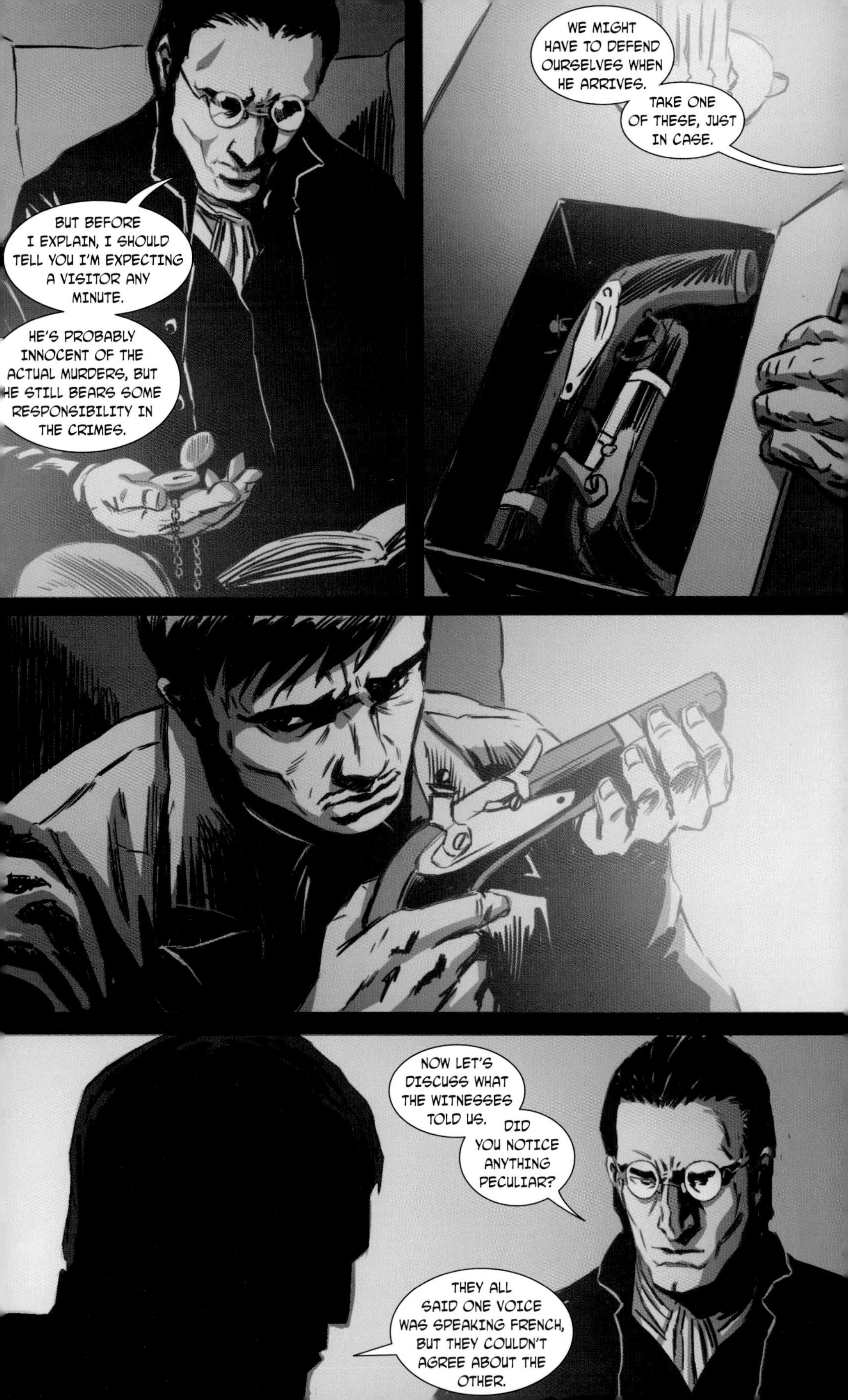
BUT BEFORE I EXPLAIN, I SHOULD TELL YOU I'M EXPECTING A VISITOR ANY MINUTE.
HE'S PROBABLY INNOCENT OF THE ACTUAL MURDERS, BUT HE STILL BEARS SOME RESPONSIBILITY IN THE CRIMES.
WE MIGHT HAVE TO DEFEND OURSELVES WHEN HE ARRIVES.
TAKE ONE OF THESE, JUST IN CASE.
NOW LET'S DISCUSS WHAT THE WITNESSES TOLD US.
DID YOU NOTICE ANYTHING PECULIAR?
THEY ALL SAID ONE VOICE WAS SPEAKING FRENCH, BUT THEY COULDN'T AGREE ABOUT THE OTHER.

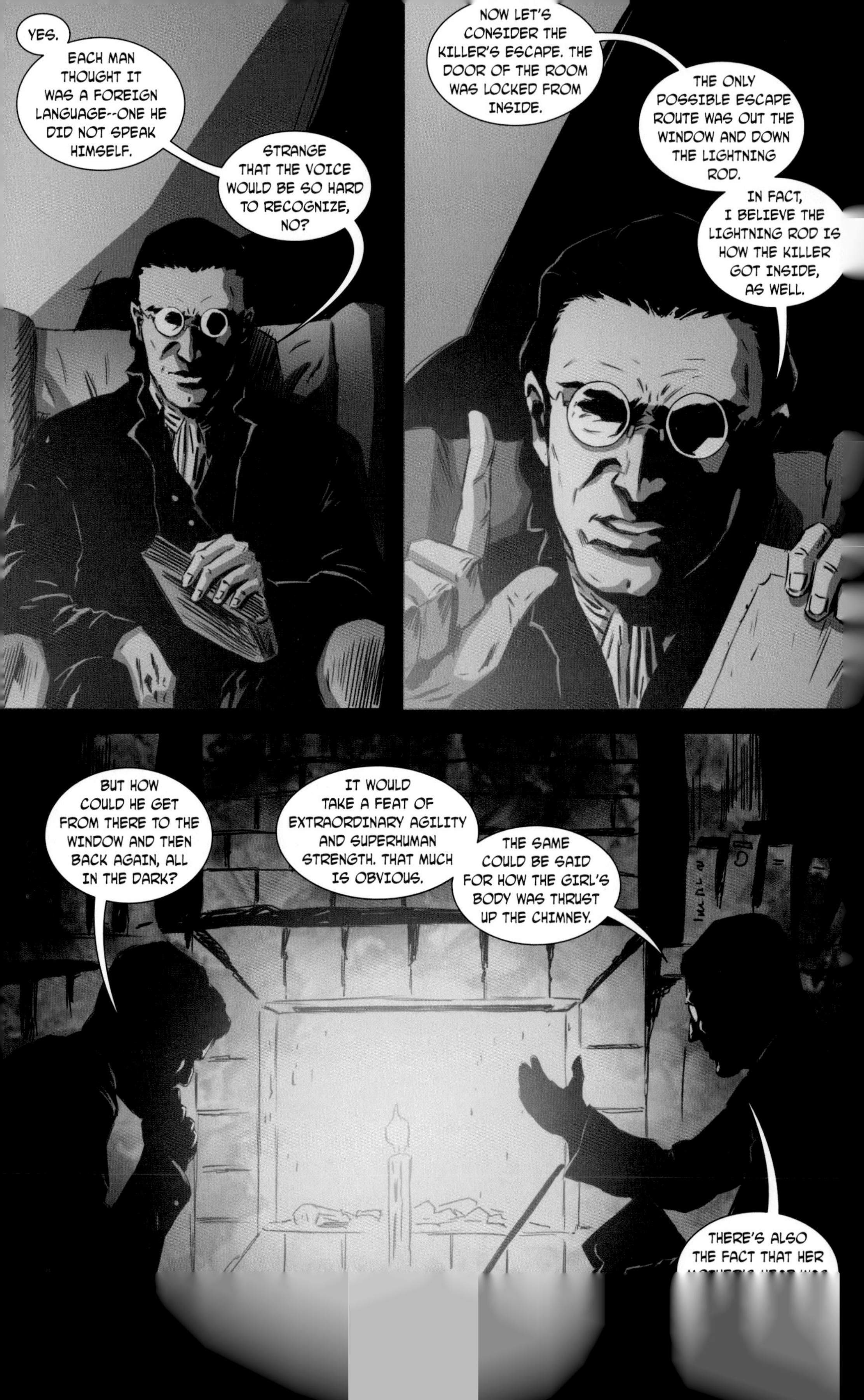
YES.
EACH MAN THOUGHT IT WAS A FOREIGN LANGUAGE--ONE HE DID NOT SPEAK HIMSELF.
STRANGE THAT THE VOICE WOULD BE SO HARD TO RECOGNIZE, NO?
NOW LET'S CONSIDER THE KILLER'S ESCAPE. THE DOOR OF THE ROOM WAS LOCKED FROM INSIDE.
THE ONLY POSSIBLE ESCAPE ROUTE WAS OUT THE WINDOW AND DOWN THE LIGHTNING ROD.
IN FACT, I BELIEVE THE LIGHTNING ROD IS HOW THE KILLER GOT INSIDE, AS WELL.
BUT HOW COULD HE GET FROM THERE TO THE WINDOW AND THEN BACK AGAIN, ALL IN THE DARK?
IT WOULD TAKE A FEAT OF EXTRAORDINARY AGILITY AND SUPERHUMAN STRENGTH. THAT MUCH IS OBVIOUS.
THE SAME COULD BE SAID FOR HOW THE GIRL'S BODY WAS THRUST UP THE CHIMNEY.
THERE'S ALSO THE FACT THAT HER

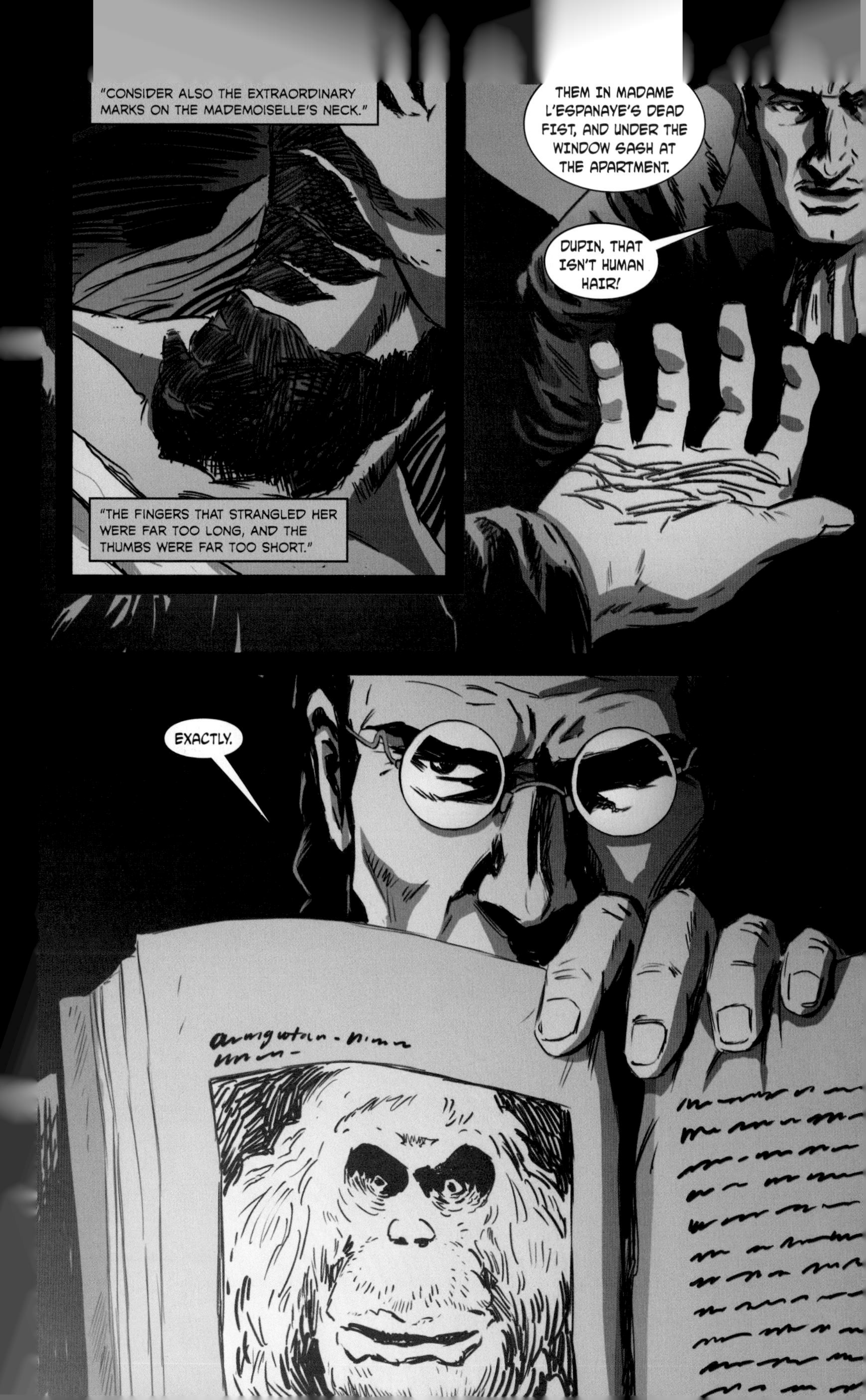
"CONSIDER ALSO THE EXTRAORDINARY MARKS ON THE MADEMOISELLE'S NECK."
"THE FINGERS THAT STRANGLED HER WERE FAR TOO LONG, AND THE THUMBS WERE FAR TOO SHORT."
THEM IN MADAME L'ESPANAYE'S DEAD FIST, AND UNDER THE WINDOW SASH AT THE APARTMENT.
DUPIN, THAT ISN'T HUMAN HAIR!
EXACTLY.

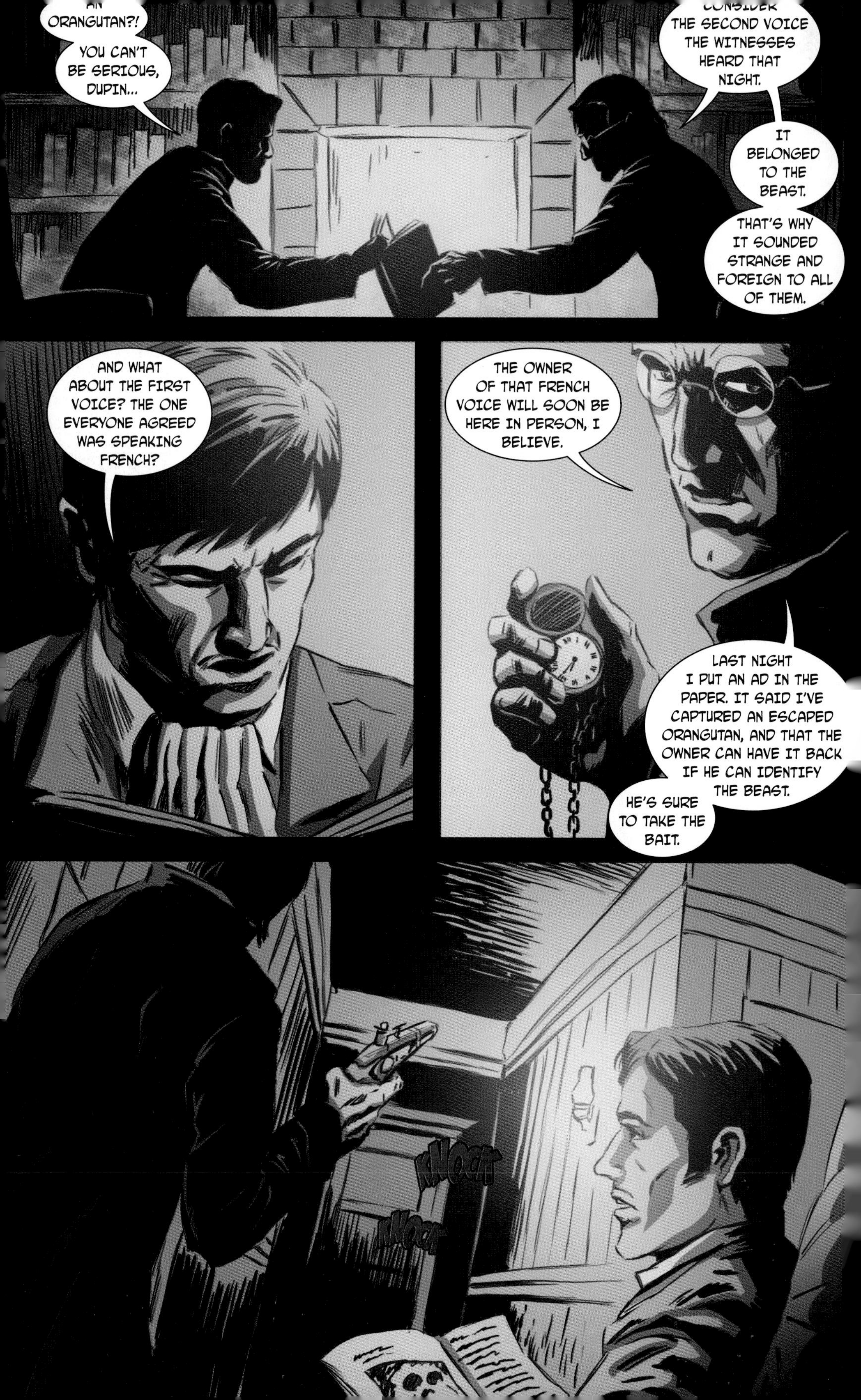
ORANGUTAN?!
YOU CAN'T BE SERIOUS, DUPIN...
THE SECOND VOICE THE WITNESSES HEARD THAT NIGHT.
IT BELONGED TO THE BEAST.
THAT'S WHY IT SOUNDED STRANGE AND FOREIGN TO ALL OF THEM.
AND WHAT ABOUT THE FIRST VOICE? THE ONE EVERYONE AGREED WAS SPEAKING FRENCH?
THE OWNER OF THAT FRENCH VOICE WILL SOON BE HERE IN PERSON, I BELIEVE.
LAST NIGHT I PUT AN AD IN THE PAPER. IT SAID I'VE CAPTURED AN ESCAPED ORANGUTAN, AND THAT THE OWNER CAN HAVE IT BACK IF HE CAN IDENTIFY THE BEAST.
HE'S SURE TO TAKE THE BAIT.
KNOCK
KNOCK

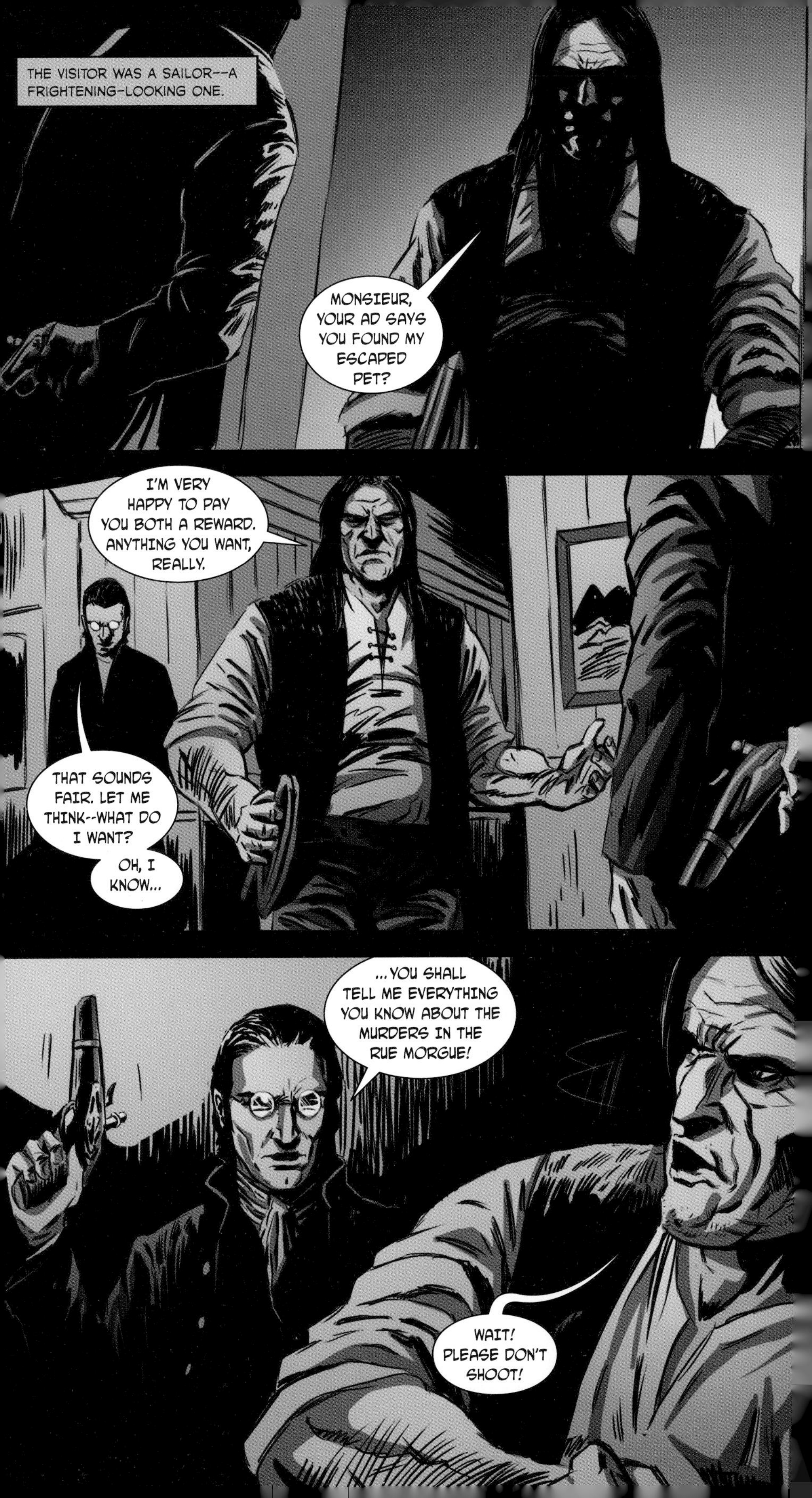
THE VISITOR WAS A SAILOR--A FRIGHTENING-LOOKING ONE.
MONSIEUR, YOUR AD SAYS YOU FOUND MY ESCAPED PET?
I'M VERY HAPPY TO PAY YOU BOTH A REWARD. ANYTHING YOU WANT, REALLY.
THAT SOUNDS FAIR. LET ME THINK--WHAT DO I WANT?
OH, I KNOW...
...YOU SHALL TELL ME EVERYTHING YOU KNOW ABOUT THE MURDERS IN THE RUE MORGUE!
WAIT! PLEASE DON'T SHOOT!

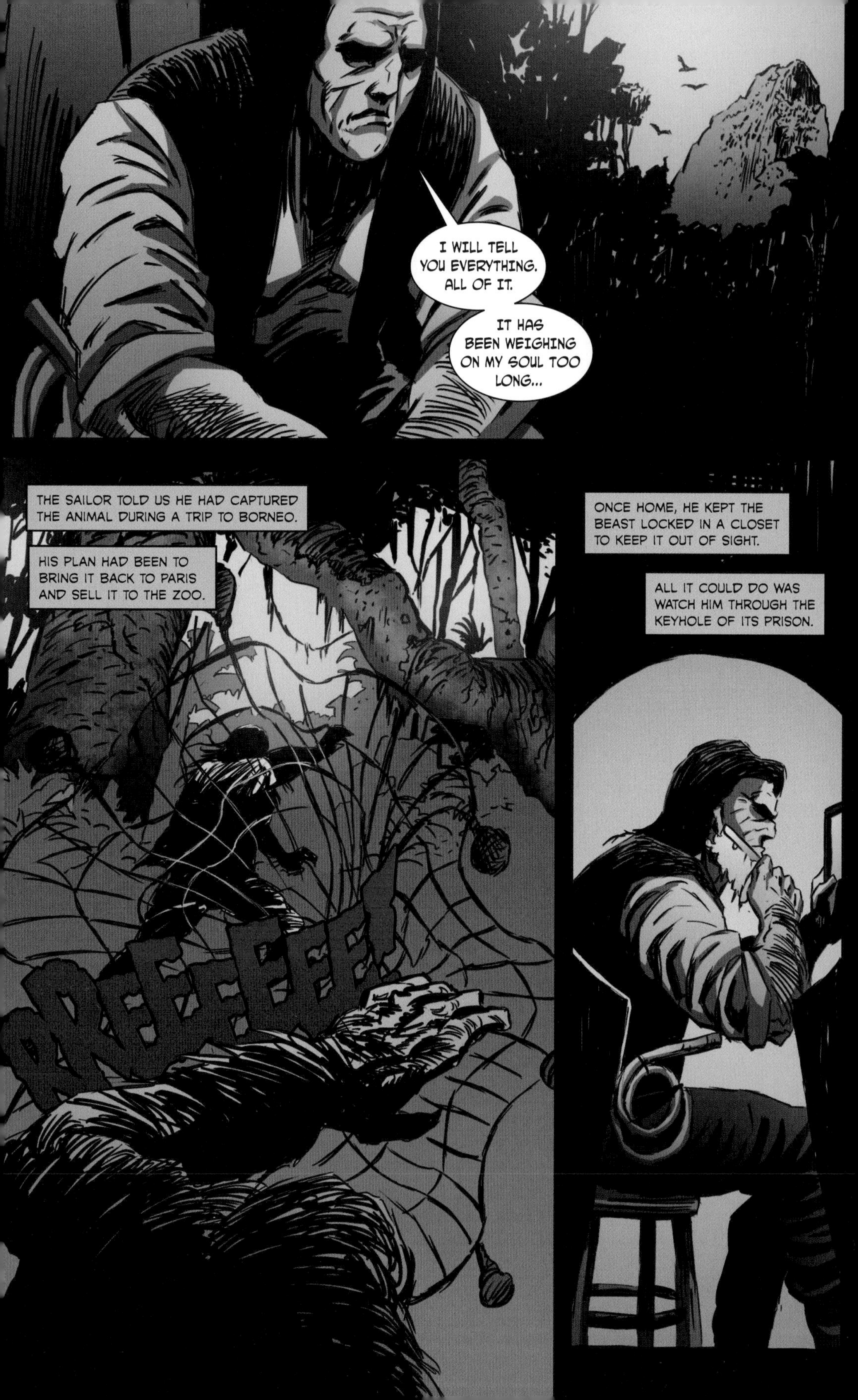
I WILL TELL YOU EVERYTHING. ALL OF IT.
IT HAS BEEN WEIGHING ON MY SOUL TOO LONG...
THE SAILOR TOLD US HE HAD CAPTURED THE ANIMAL DURING A TRIP TO BORNEO.
HIS PLAN HAD BEEN TO BRING IT BACK TO PARIS AND SELL IT TO THE ZOO.
ONCE HOME, HE KEPT THE BEAST LOCKED IN A CLOSET TO KEEP IT OUT OF SIGHT.
ALL IT COULD DO WAS WATCH HIM THROUGH THE KEYHOLE OF ITS PRISON.

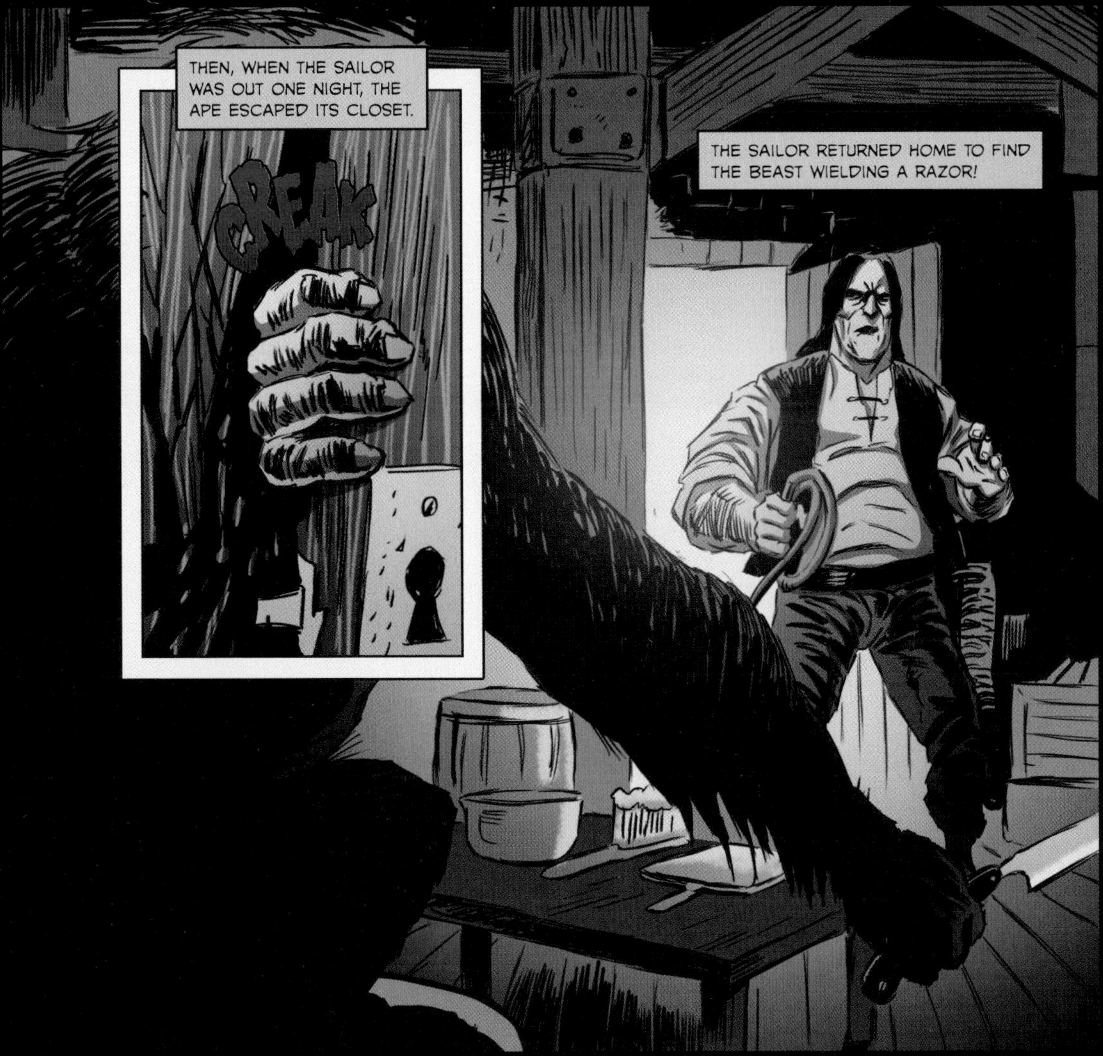
THEN, WHEN THE SAILOR WAS OUT ONE NIGHT, THE APE ESCAPED ITS CLOSET.
CREAK
THE SAILOR RETURNED HOME TO FIND THE BEAST WIELDING A RAZOR!

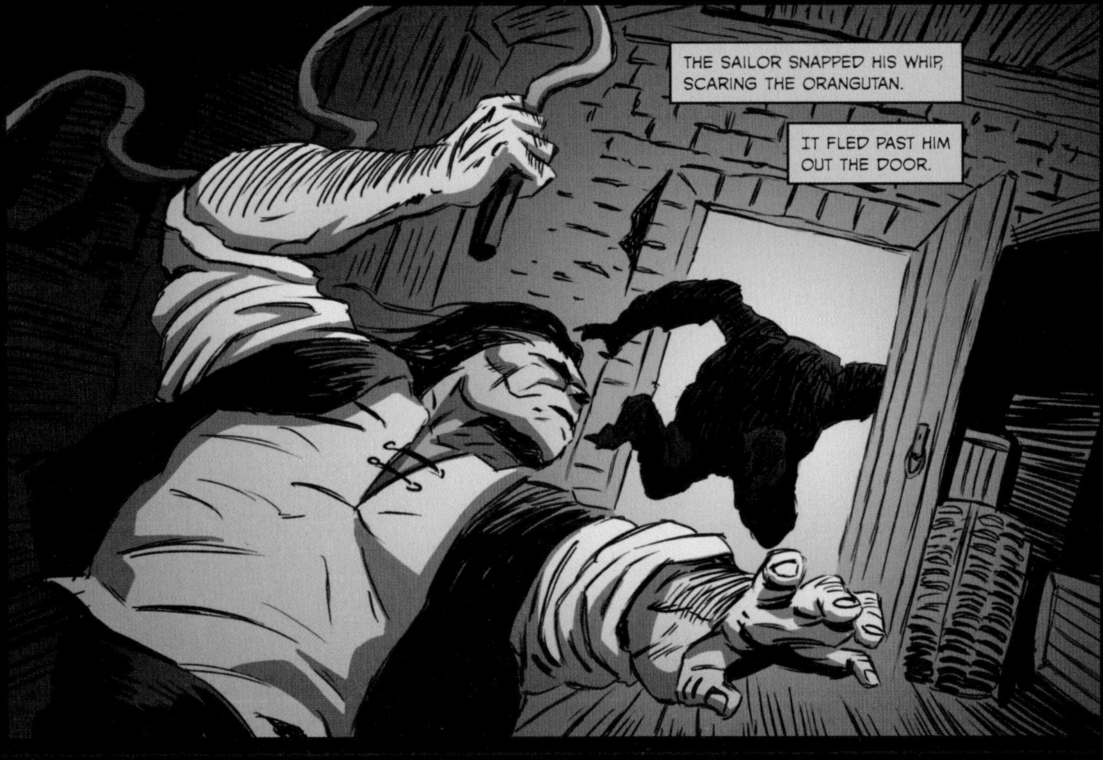
THE SAILOR SNAPPED HIS WHIP, SCARING THE ORANGUTAN.
IT FLED PAST HIM OUT THE DOOR.

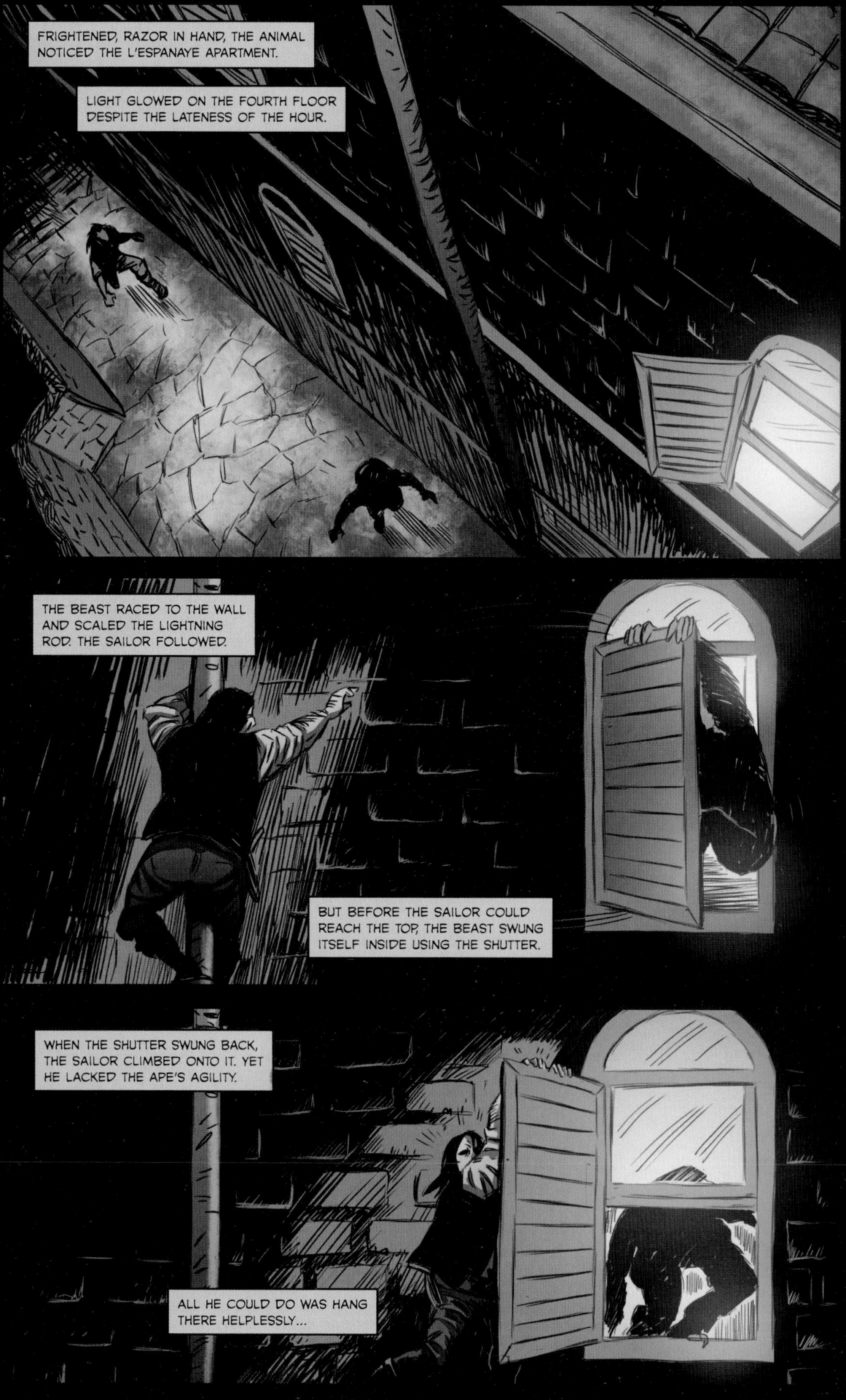

FRIGHTENED, RAZOR IN HAND, THE ANIMAL NOTICED THE L'ESPANAYE APARTMENT.
LIGHT GLOWED ON THE FOURTH FLOOR DESPITE THE LATENESS OF THE HOUR.
THE BEAST RACED TO THE WALL AND SCALED THE LIGHTNING ROD. THE SAILOR FOLLOWED.
BUT BEFORE THE SAILOR COULD REACH THE TOP, THE BEAST SWUNG ITSELF INSIDE USING THE SHUTTER.
WHEN THE SHUTTER SWUNG BACK, THE SAILOR CLIMBED ONTO IT. YET HE LACKED THE APE'S AGILITY.
ALL HE COULD DO WAS HANG THERE HELPLESSLY...

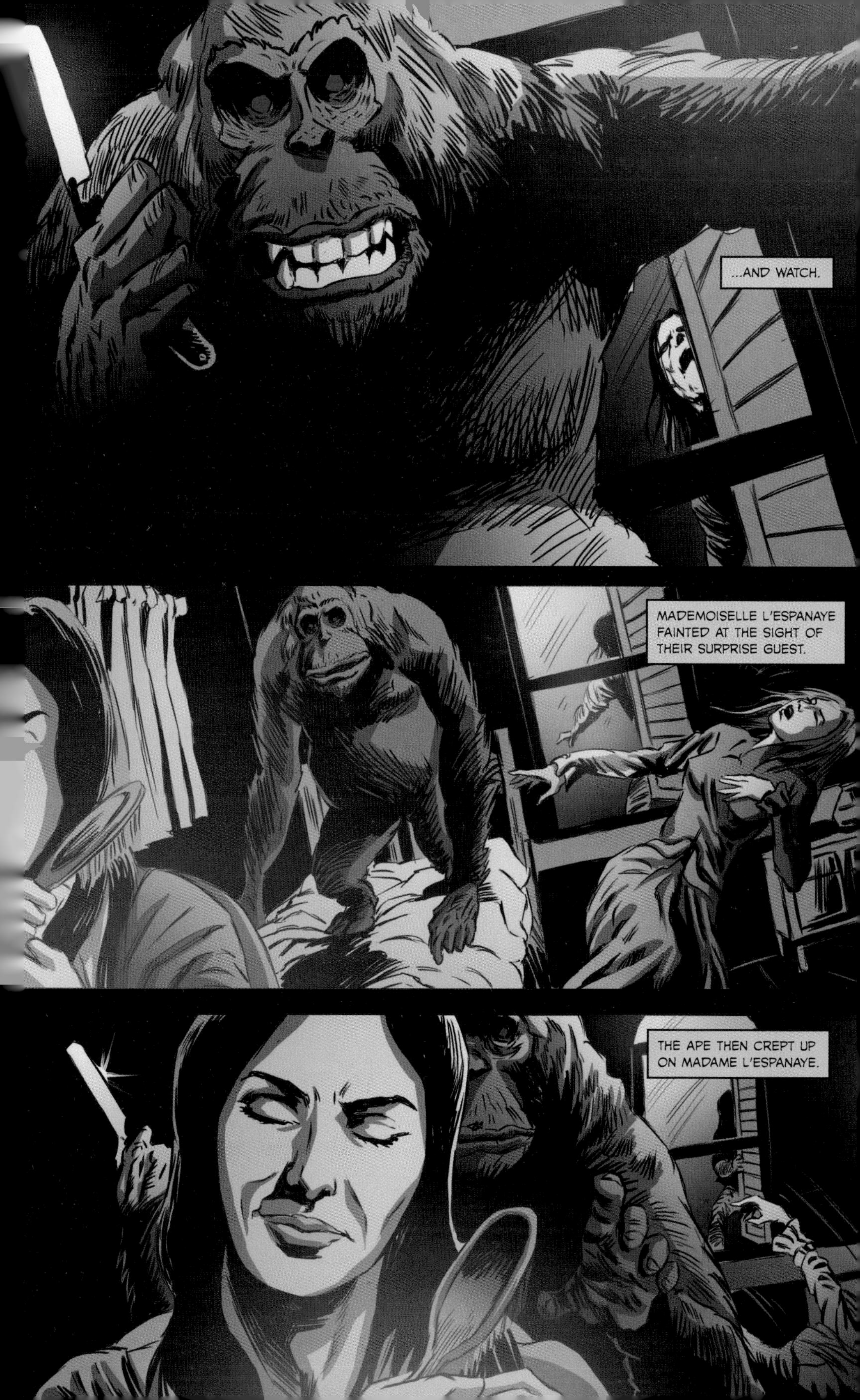
...AND WATCH.
MADEMOISELLE L'ESPANAYE FAINTED AT THE SIGHT OF THEIR SURPRISE GUEST.
THE APE THEN CREPT UP ON MADAME L'ESPANAYE.

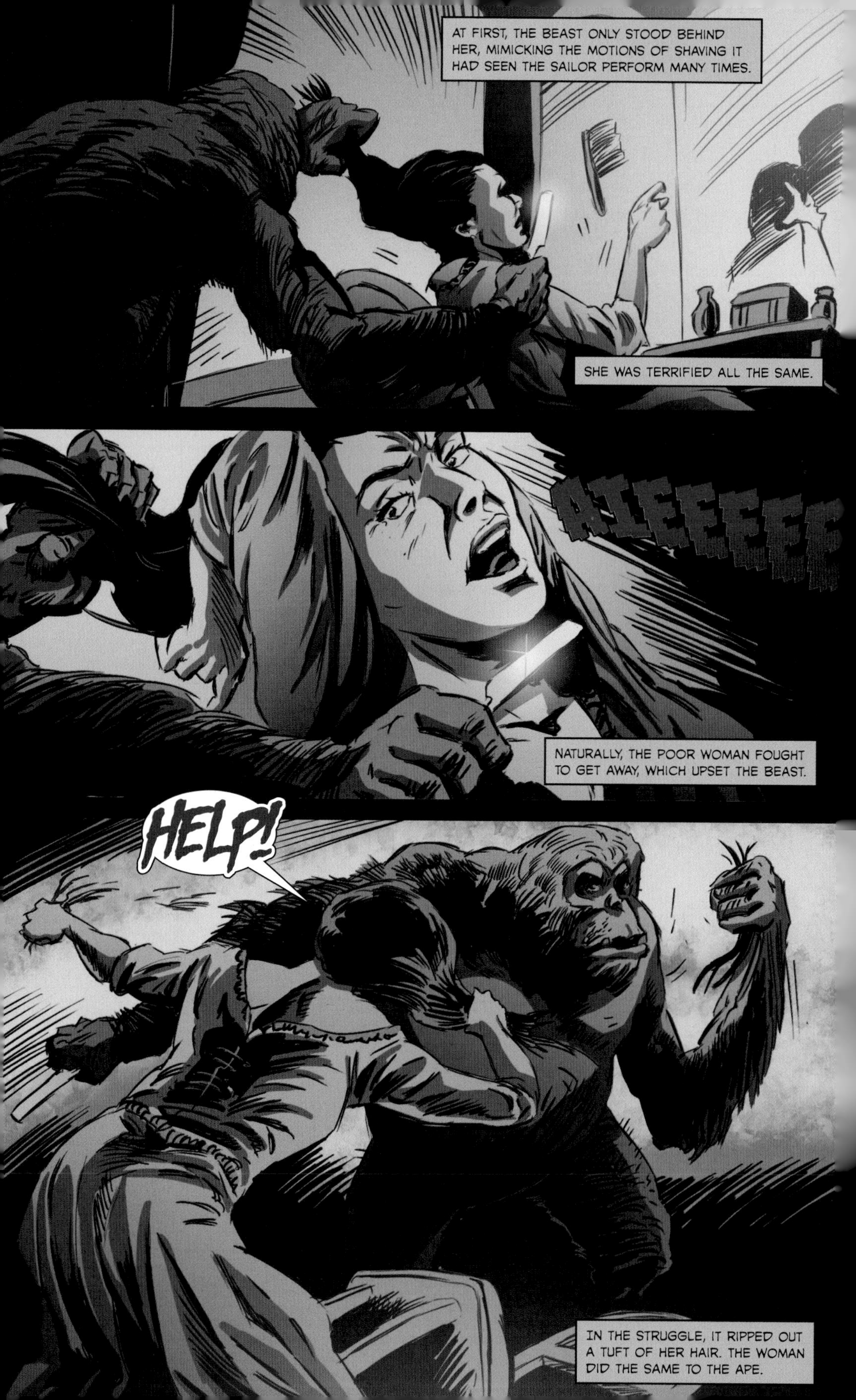
AT FIRST, THE BEAST ONLY STOOD BEHIND HER, MIMICKING THE MOTIONS OF SHAVING IT HAD SEEN THE SAILOR PERFORM MANY TIMES.
SHE WAS TERRIFIED ALL THE SAME.
AIEEEEEE
NATURALLY, THE POOR WOMAN FOUGHT TO GET AWAY, WHICH UPSET THE BEAST.
HELP!
IN THE STRUGGLE, IT RIPPED OUT A TUFT OF HER HAIR. THE WOMAN DID THE SAME TO THE APE.

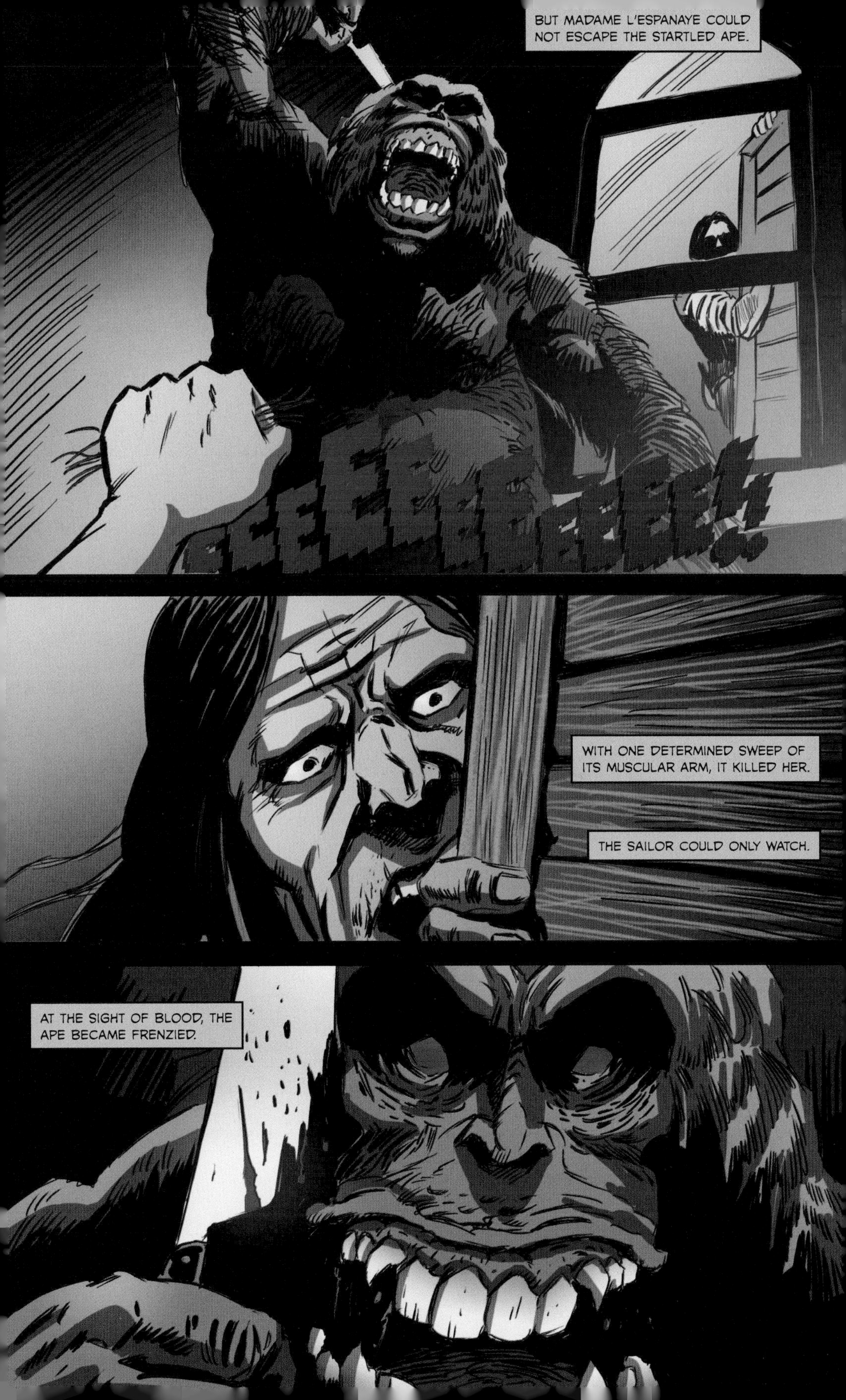
BUT MADAME L'ESPANAYE COULD NOT ESCAPE THE STARTLED APE.
WITH ONE DETERMINED SWEEP OF ITS MUSCULAR ARM, IT KILLED HER.
THE SAILOR COULD ONLY WATCH.
AT THE SIGHT OF BLOOD, THE APE BECAME FRENZIED.

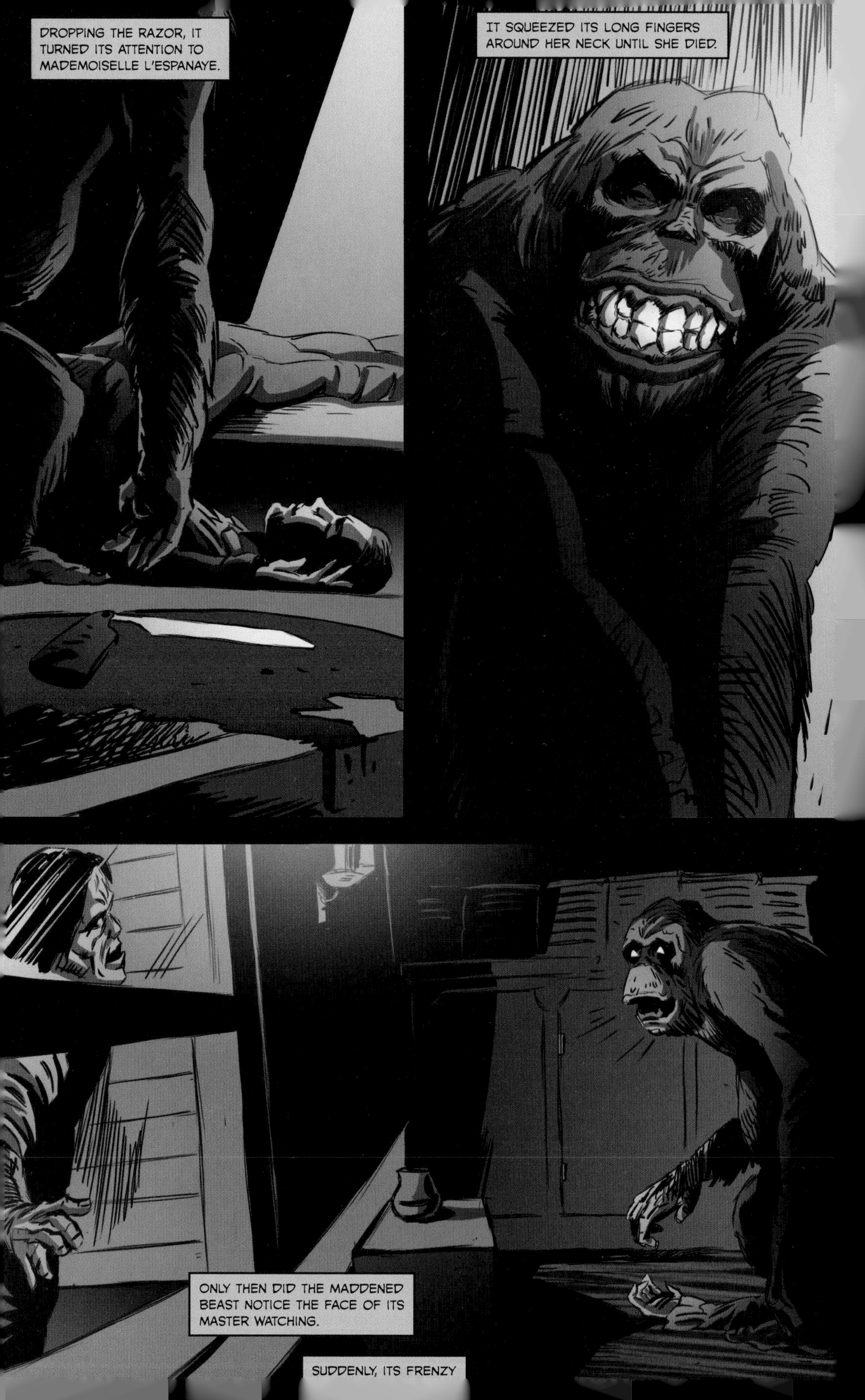
DROPPING THE RAZOR, IT TURNED ITS ATTENTION TO MADEMOISELLE L'ESPANAYE.
IT SQUEEZED ITS LONG FINGERS AROUND HER NECK UNTIL SHE DIED.
ONLY THEN DID THE MADDENED BEAST NOTICE THE FACE OF ITS MASTER WATCHING.
SUDDENLY, ITS FRENZY

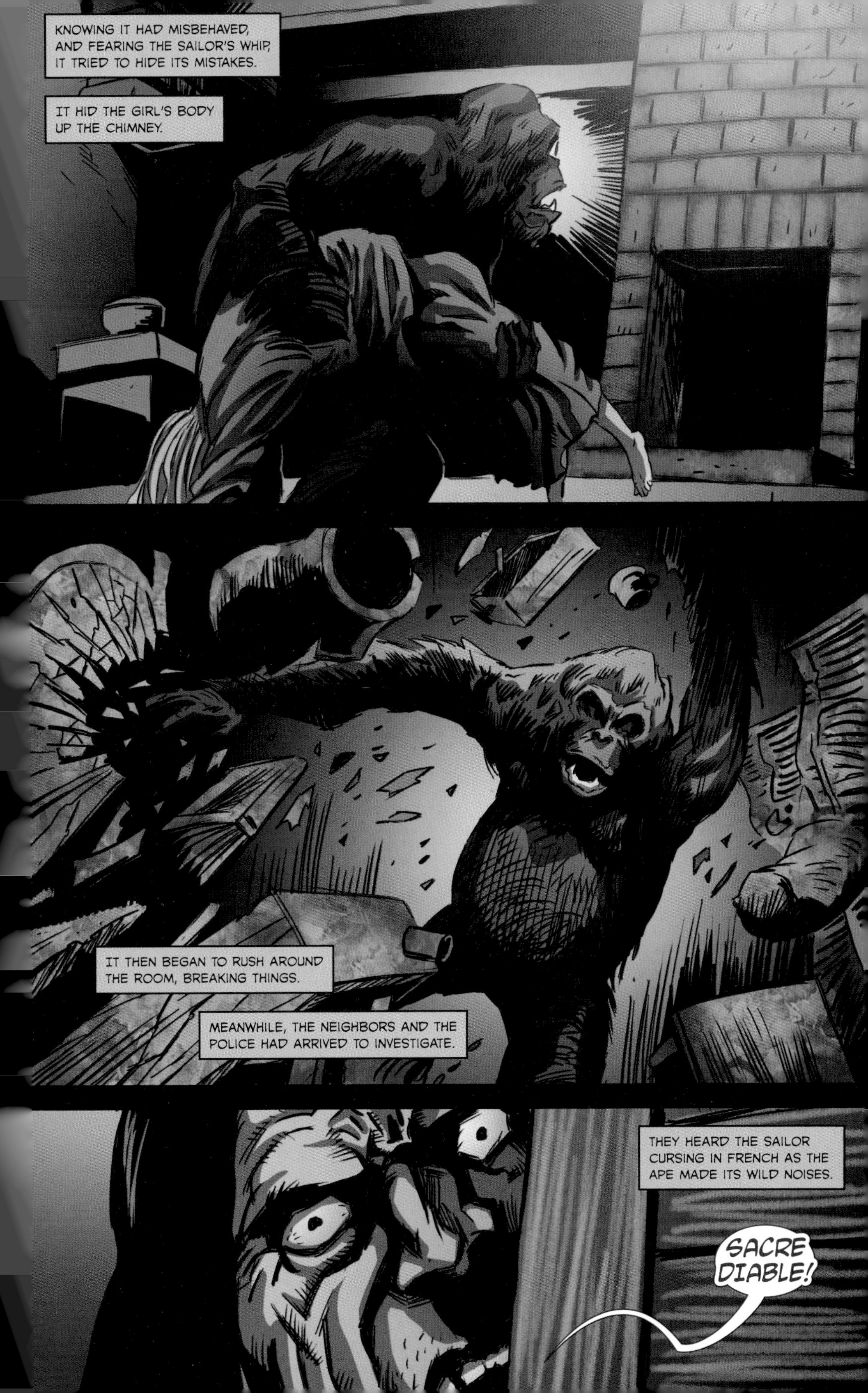
KNOWING IT HAD MISBEHAVED, AND FEARING THE SAILOR'S WHIP, IT TRIED TO HIDE ITS MISTAKES.
IT HID THE GIRL'S BODY UP THE CHIMNEY.
IT THEN BEGAN TO RUSH AROUND THE ROOM, BREAKING THINGS.
MEANWHILE, THE NEIGHBORS AND THE POLICE HAD ARRIVED TO INVESTIGATE.
THEY HEARD THE SAILOR CURSING IN FRENCH AS THE APE MADE ITS WILD NOISES.
SACRE DIABLE!

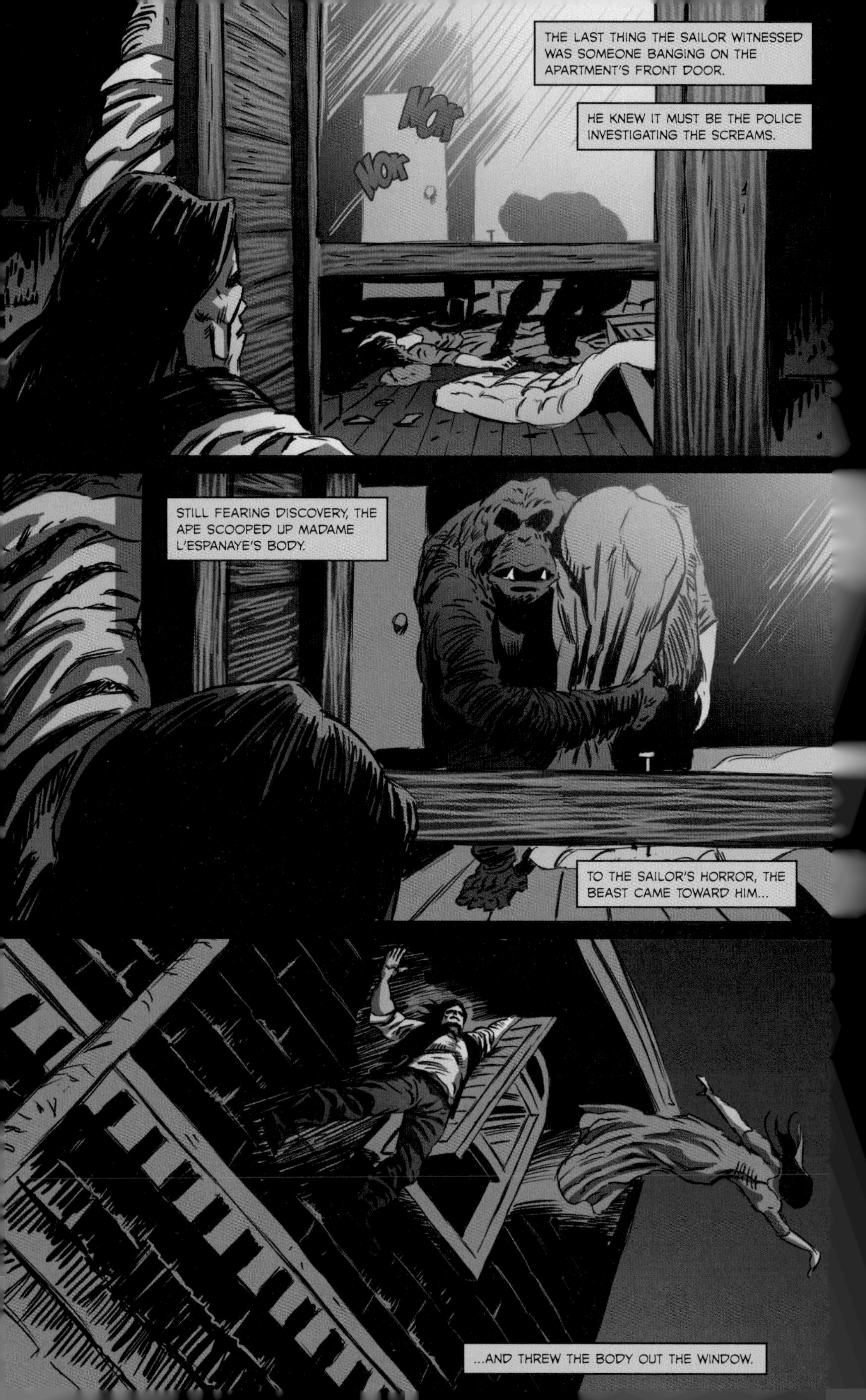
THE LAST THING THE SAILOR WITNESSED WAS SOMEONE BANGING ON THE APARTMENT'S FRONT DOOR.
HE KNEW IT MUST BE THE POLICE INVESTIGATING THE SCREAMS.
NOK
NOK
STILL FEARING DISCOVERY, THE APE SCOOPED UP MADAME L'ESPANAYE'S BODY.
TO THE SAILOR'S HORROR, THE BEAST CAME TOWARD HIM...
...AND THREW THE BODY OUT THE WINDOW.

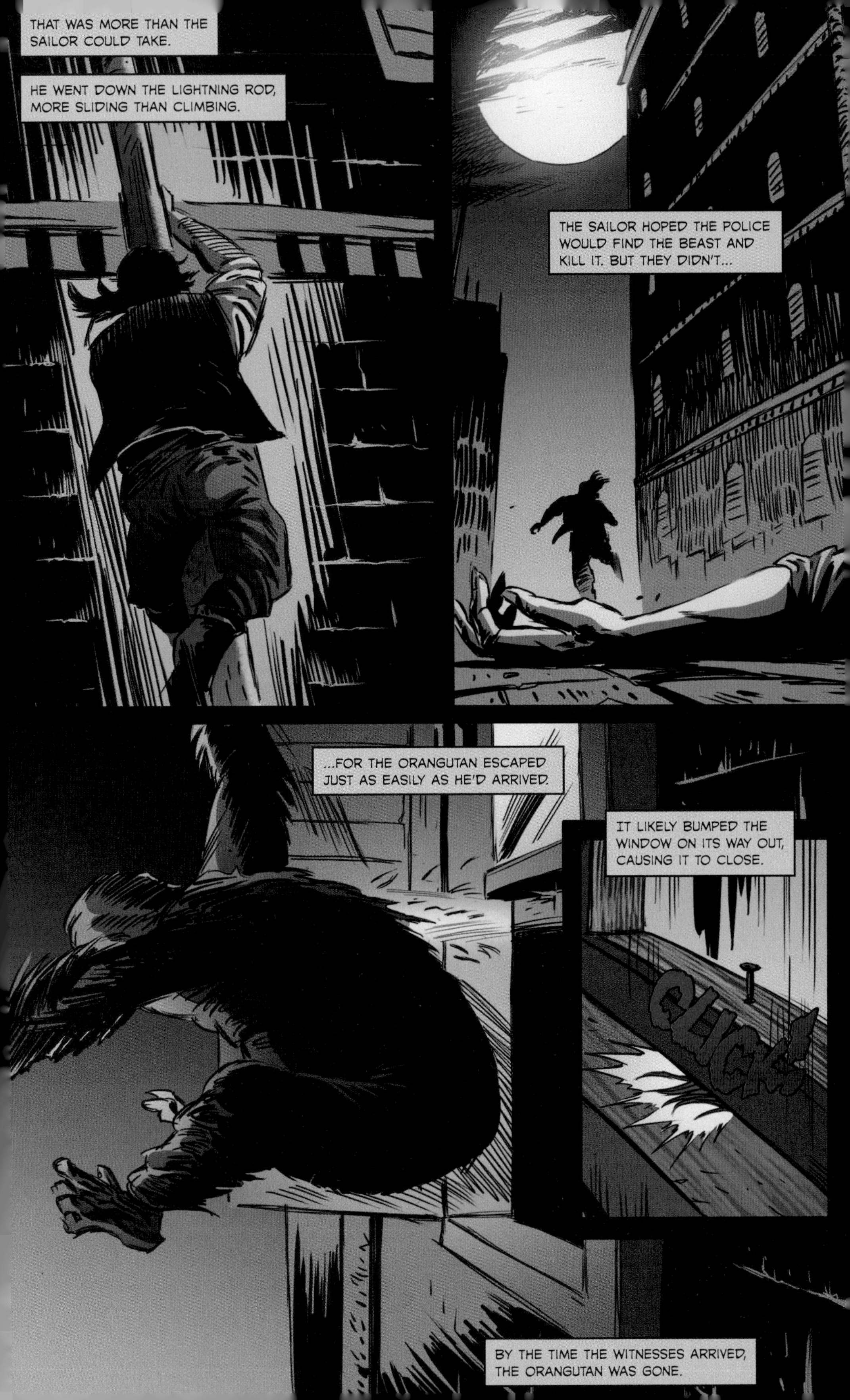
THAT WAS MORE THAN THE SAILOR COULD TAKE.
HE WENT DOWN THE LIGHTNING ROD, MORE SLIDING THAN CLIMBING.
THE SAILOR HOPED THE POLICE WOULD FIND THE BEAST AND KILL IT. BUT THEY DIDN'T...
...FOR THE ORANGUTAN ESCAPED JUST AS EASILY AS HE'D ARRIVED.
IT LIKELY BUMPED THE WINDOW ON ITS WAY OUT, CAUSING IT TO CLOSE.
CLICK!
BY THE TIME THE WITNESSES ARRIVED, THE ORANGUTAN WAS GONE.

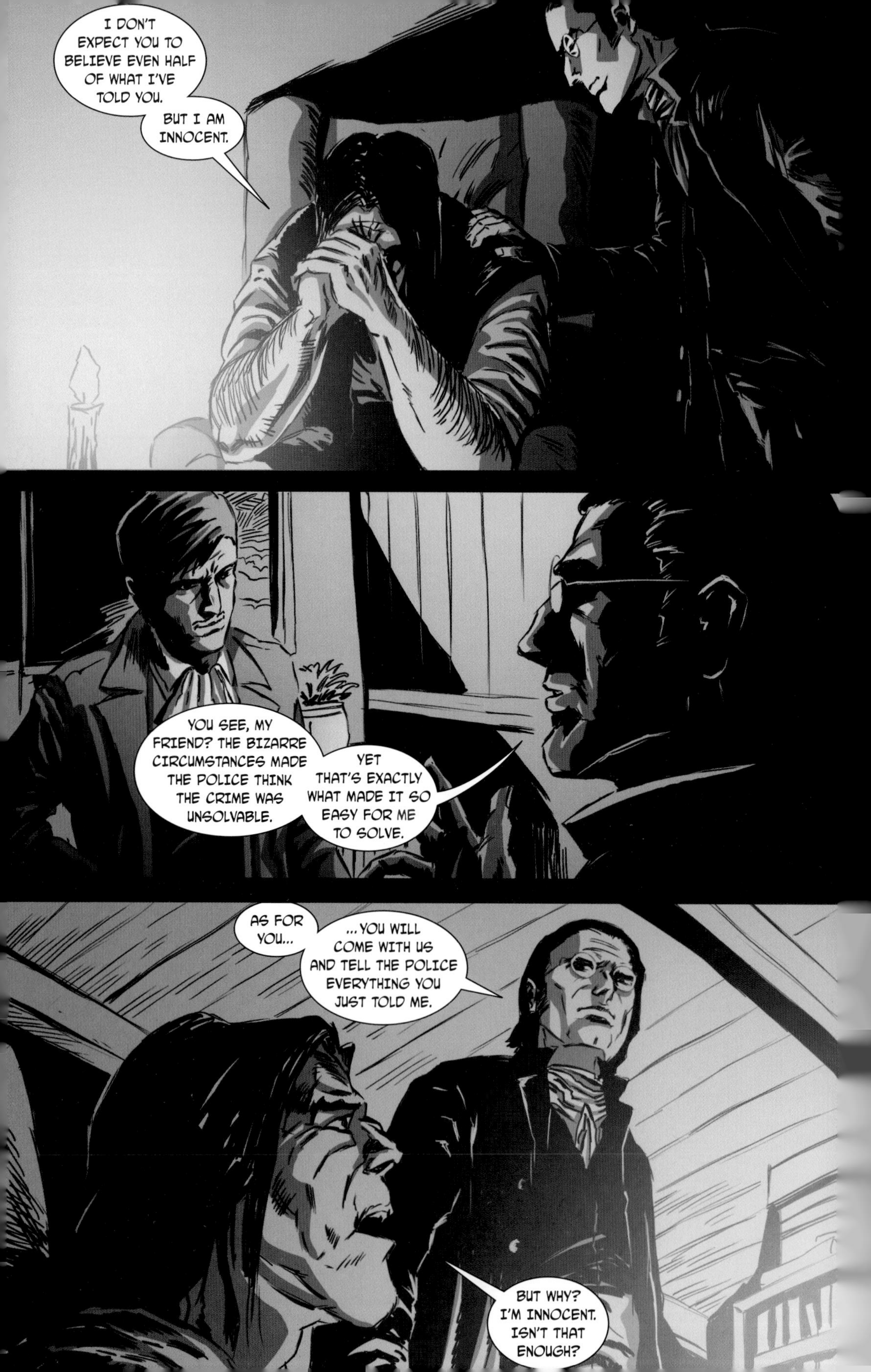
I DON'T EXPECT YOU TO BELIEVE EVEN HALF OF WHAT I'VE TOLD YOU.
BUT I AM INNOCENT.
YOU SEE, MY FRIEND? THE BIZARRE CIRCUMSTANCES MADE THE POLICE THINK THE CRIME WAS UNSOLVABLE.
YET THAT'S EXACTLY WHAT MADE IT SO EASY FOR ME TO SOLVE.
AS FOR YOU...
...YOU WILL COME WITH US AND TELL THE POLICE EVERYTHING YOU JUST TOLD ME.
BUT WHY? I'M INNOCENT. ISN'T THAT ENOUGH?

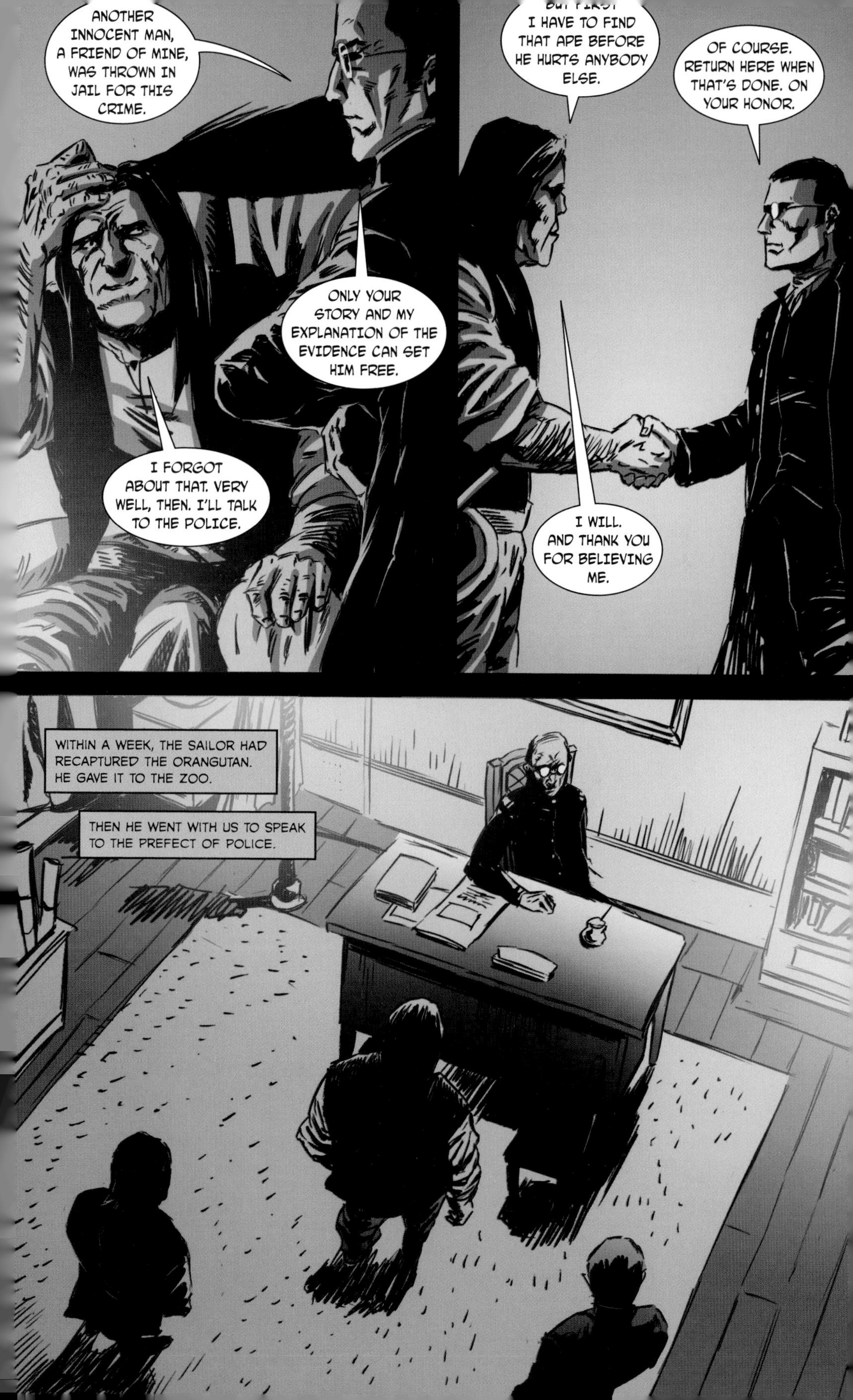
ANOTHER INNOCENT MAN, A FRIEND OF MINE, WAS THROWN IN JAIL FOR THIS CRIME.
ONLY YOUR STORY AND MY EXPLANATION OF THE EVIDENCE CAN SET HIM FREE.
I FORGOT ABOUT THAT. VERY WELL, THEN. I'LL TALK TO THE POLICE.
I HAVE TO FIND THAT APE BEFORE HE HURTS ANYBODY ELSE.
OF COURSE. RETURN HERE WHEN THAT'S DONE. ON YOUR HONOR.
I WILL. AND THANK YOU FOR BELIEVING ME.
WITHIN A WEEK, THE SAILOR HAD RECAPTURED THE ORANGUTAN. HE GAVE IT TO THE ZOO.
THEN HE WENT WITH US TO SPEAK TO THE PREFECT OF POLICE.

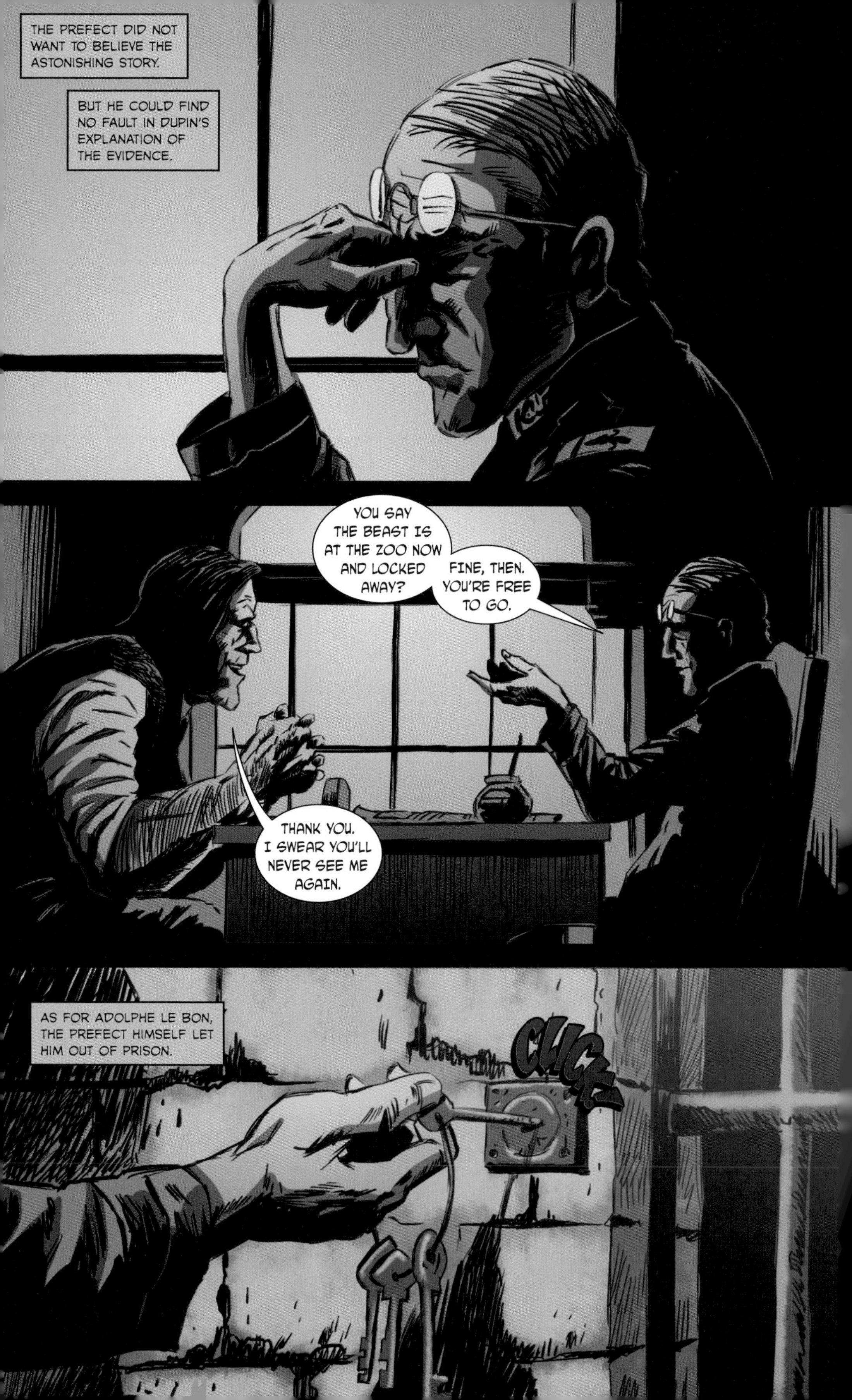
THE PREFECT DID NOT WANT TO BELIEVE THE ASTONISHING STORY.
BUT HE COULD FIND NO FAULT IN DUPIN'S EXPLANATION OF THE EVIDENCE.
YOU SAY THE BEAST IS AT THE ZOO NOW AND LOCKED AWAY?
FINE, THEN. YOU'RE FREE TO GO.
THANK YOU. I SWEAR YOU'LL NEVER SEE ME AGAIN.
AS FOR ADOLPHE LE BON, THE PREFECT HIMSELF LET HIM OUT OF PRISON.
CLICK

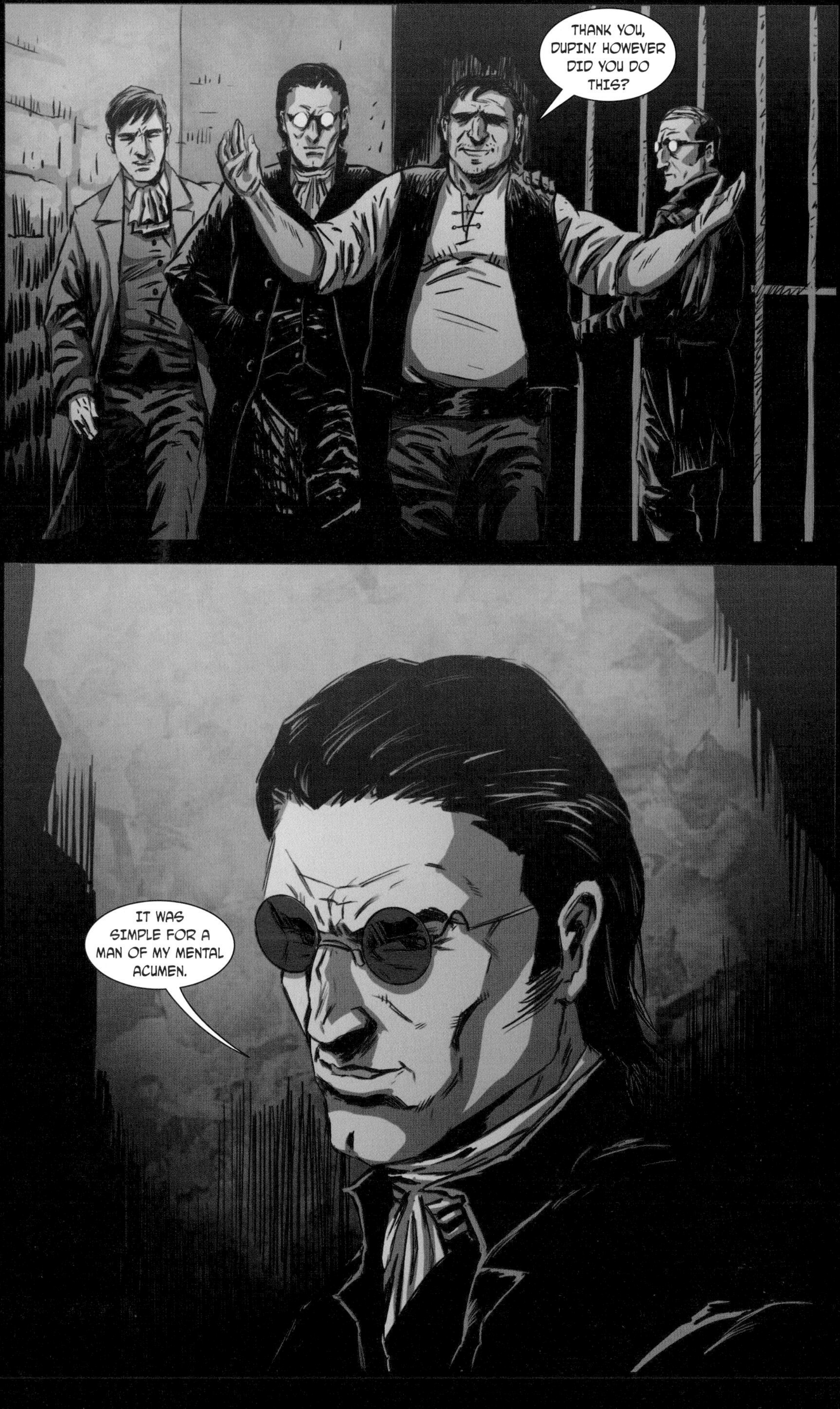
THANK YOU, DUPIN! HOWEVER DID YOU DO THIS?
IT WAS SIMPLE FOR A MAN OF MY MENTAL ACUMEN.

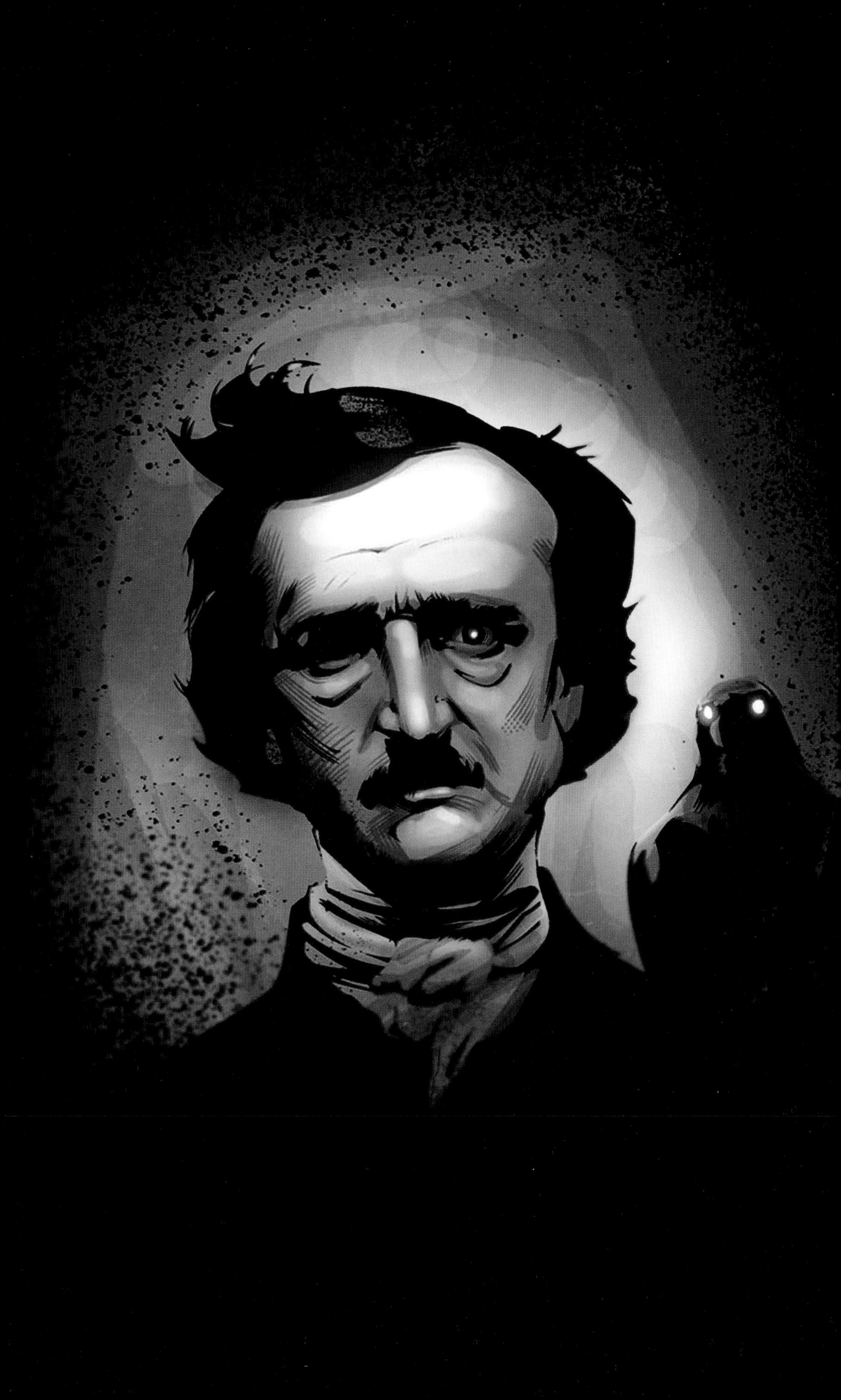

Over the course of his life, Edgar Allan Poe submitted many stories and poems to a number of publications. All of them were either rejected, or he received little to no compensation for them. His most popular work, "The Raven", quite nearly made him a household name--but only earned him nine dollars.

Poe was unable to hold a single job for very long, jumping from position to position for most of his life. He had very few friends, was in constant financial trouble, and struggled with alcoholism throughout his adult years. Edgar's family rarely helped him during these difficult times. In fact, when Edgar's father died in 1834, he did not even mention Edgar in his will.

Though largely unappreciated in his own lifetime, Edgar Allan Poe is now recognized as one of the most important writers of American literature.

THE RETELLING AUTHOR

CARL BOWEN is a father, husband, and writer living in Lawrenceville, Georgia. He was born in Louisiana, lived briefly in England, and was raised in Georgia where he went to school. He has published a handful of novels, short stories, and comics. For Stone Arch Books, he has retold *20,000 Leagues Under the Sea*, *The Strange Case of Dr. Jekyll and Mr. Hyde*, *The Jungle Book*, *Aladdin and the Magic Lamp*, *Julius Caesar* (by William Shakespeare) and this comic book. He is the original author of *BMX Breakthrough* as well as the Shadow Squadron series—which includes *Sea Demon*, *Black Anchor*, *Eagle Down*, and *Sniper Shield*.

THE ILLUSTRATOR

EMERSON DIMAYA makes banner ads and websites by day, and illustrates comics by night. His tools of the trade include pencils, pens, and computer applications like photoshop, illustrator, and Corel Draw. His dark, moody, and atmospheric style of illustration is inspired by his fascination with zombies, monsters, and other supernatural creatures. He is currently living with his wife and a dog on an island somewhere in the Philippines.

GLOSSARY

ACUMEN *(AK-yoo-muhn)*--keen insight or intellect

AGILITY *(uh-JIL-i-tee)*--the power of moving quickly and easily

ASTONISHING *(uh-STON-ish-ing)*--surprising and impressive

BIZARRE *(bi-ZAR)*--very strange or odd

CONTRARY *(KON-trer-ee)*--opposite

CREPT *(KREPT)*--moved slowly and silently

EXTRAORDINARY *(ek-STROR-duh-ner-ee)*--very unusual or remarkable

FRANCS *(FRANGKZ)*--the main unit of money in Switzerland, many African countries, and formerly in France

LINGERED *(LING-gurd)*--stayed or waited around

MORGUE *(MORG)*--a place in which bodies are kept, especially the bodies of victims of violence, crimes, or accidents

PREFECT *(PREE-fekt)*--a person appointed to any of several command positions, like the chief administrative official of a department in France

RECOGNIZE *(REK-uhg-nize)*--to see or hear someone and know who that person is

SECLUDED *(si-KLOO-did)*--quiet and private, as in a secluded valley

SHRILL *(SHRIL)*--having a high, sharp, or harsh sound

SYMPATHY *(SIM-puh-thee)*--the understanding and sharing of other people's troubles

VISUAL QUESTIONS

1. What do the lines next to the orangutan's face mean? What is he thinking? (If you're not sure, check page 57 for clues.)

2. Why do you think the window, the body outline, and Dupin's glasses are red in this spread? What do you think is the purpose of the red color accent throughout the book?

3. Based on what you know from the story, whose voice is saying "Sacre Diable!" in this panel?

4. Why are the orangutan's eyes red in the left panel, and white in the right panel? Why do you think the creators chose to do this? Check pages 52–57 for hints.

5. Dupin is a very intelligent man. Identify several panels in this book where he shows his impressive attention to detail, keen intelligence, or amazing acumen.

THE FALL OF THE HOUSE OF USHER

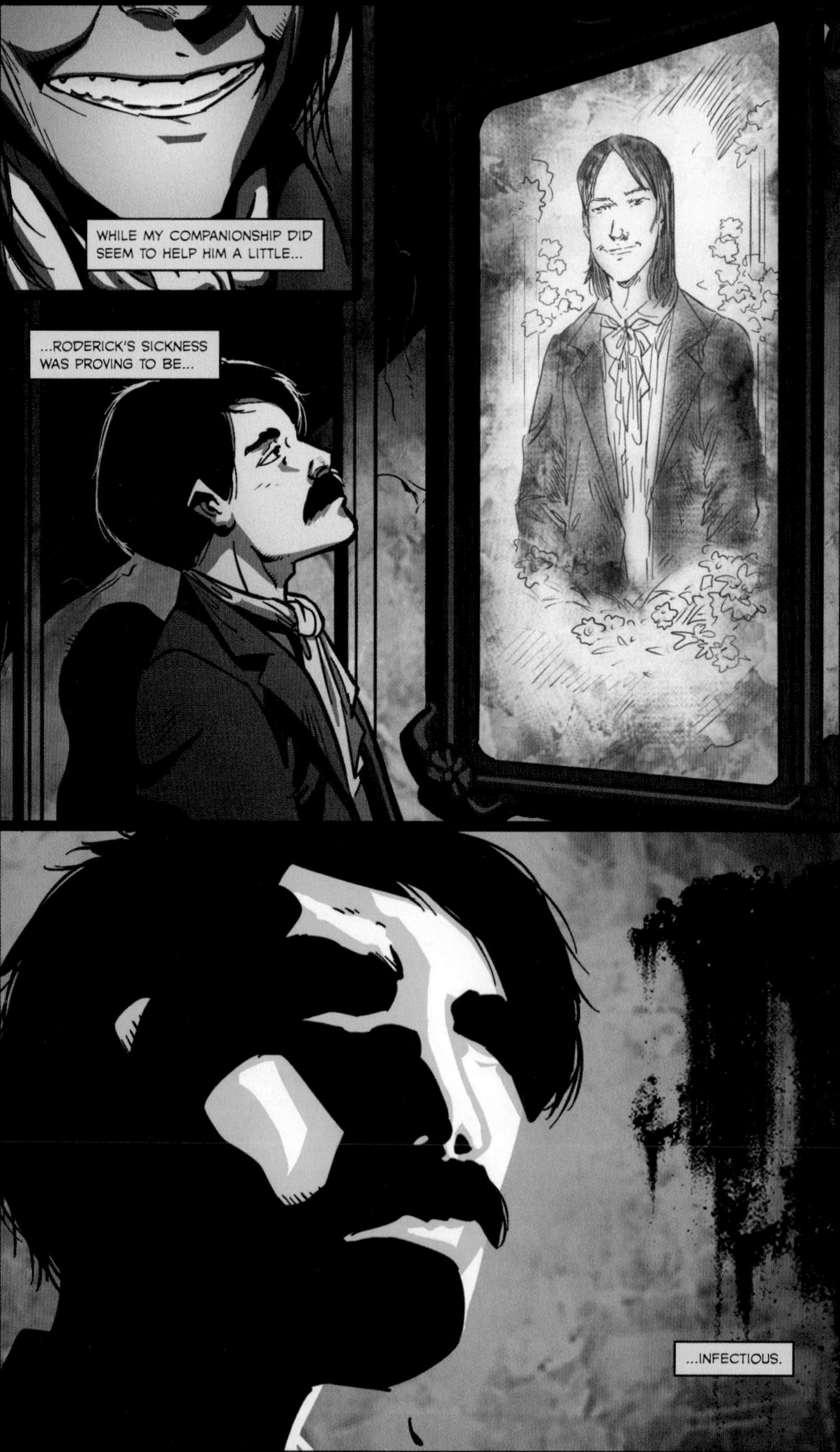
WHILE MY COMPANIONSHIP DID SEEM TO HELP HIM A LITTLE...
...RODERICK'S SICKNESS WAS PROVING TO BE...
...INFECTIOUS.

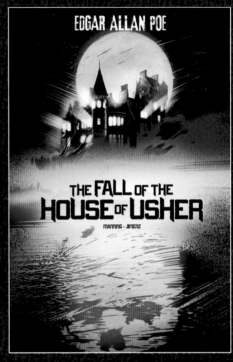
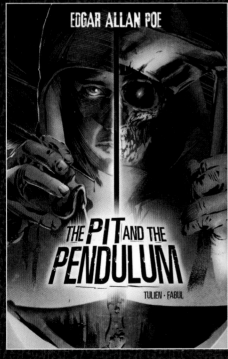
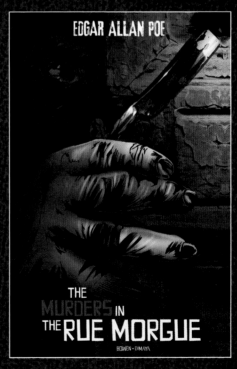